I0721357

CHAPTER ONE

I THOUGHT IT was a plane.

It was metallic and shiny and came out of storm clouds low and obviously in trouble though, to be honest, I didn't actually see it. Just a glimpse from the corner of my eye because I was focused on changing a flat tire on a remote, lonely road in the middle of nowhere while watching storm clouds advance and hoping to get back on the road before the storm made reaching the highway impossible.

Turned out it wasn't a plane, but I didn't learn that until later.

The tire had been put on with an impact wrench which meant a mere human couldn't get it off with mere human strength so I was close to panic because those clouds were roiling and dark and menacing and the storm they were bringing would last for days with a drop in temperature that would make survival dependent on curling up in the car wearing every bit of clothes in my suitcase.

So, I was determined to get that tire off and it took the sound of the crash to break my concentration as that shiny thing plowed into the cliff directly above me. Then I remembered the metallic shine of a plane. Dear God, let the people be okay. Looking towards the sound, I saw that shine again, only now it was embedded in the side of the mountain. A really bad crash. The worst. And a storm was coming fast.

Then something happened that made me forget both crash and flat tire. A subtle sound at first – a rumble -- that was as much a feeling of the ground shaking as an actual sound. Then the side of the mountain just below the crash site moved and started to slide. I watched in fascination because it resembled a living thing, slipping and weaving and gathering speed as it started downward.

Towards me.

It took seconds to realize what it was. A landslide. An avalanche. Panic took over. I ran for my life full tilt towards the forest that grew close to the dirt road I'd decided to take because all those trees were lovely and I was in no hurry, having left home in plenty of time to reach college before the summer session began. Who'd have thought there'd be a late spring blizzard or that I'd have a flat tire?

I made it to safety. The landslide thundered past with only a few stray rocks hitting my legs as I ran. Then the mountain settled back into its usual, quiet majesty. But what moments earlier had been a road with my car on it was now rubble.

No road.

No car.

Just a pile of dirt with a deadly late winter storm

approaching and me in a light jacket suitable for a warm, spring afternoon with everything I owned buried beneath that pile of dirt.

As I tried to take in what had just happened -- and what new danger I was now facing -- the first flakes of the coming blizzard fell, huge, white beautiful snowflakes touching my face and arms before melting because the cold hadn't reached me yet. But it would.

As the lowering clouds came closer and then closer still, I forced my mind to think ahead because in mere minutes the storm would envelop me, and I'd freeze to death unless I could come up with some way to survive.

I didn't want to die. But the possibility was very real. I doubled over and almost retched.

The sun still shone where the snow hadn't reached the crash site yet. The metal of the crashed plane winked brightly. I stared at that shiny metal. The inside of that plane would be warm. It was my best bet to survive the coming storm.

So without hesitating I began the climb up the side of the mountain along the side of the ugly slash of the avalanche's path, aiming for that glint of silver that could mean the difference between life and death.

Then the storm hit in all its fury. Huge flakes turned the world white and made seeing more than a few feet impossible and the cold wrapped me in an icy blanket. I started shivering and soon I couldn't stop. I wanted to sit down and hug myself to keep warm but I knew that would be suicide.

So, I followed the scar left by the avalanche and, since the plane crash had obviously caused it, I knew that when I reached the top of the scar, I'd also reach the plane and safety. If it was still in one piece and I refused to think otherwise. I climbed one step at a time. And one more. And one more after that. Surely, I told myself, the plane was only one step away. But then I'd have to take another step.

The snowflakes were so thick that I actually walked smack into the side of the plane. I ran a hand along the smooth metal looking for a door or window. I shouted but no one answered. Perhaps they were dead? I put aside the thought of dead bodies as I felt my way along the side of the plane looking for a way inside.

It was a large plane. It was long and smooth, and I couldn't discern its shape and decided it must be a freighter because there were no windows. But there had to be a door. Somewhere.

I kept moving, feeling my way as the snowflakes grew thicker and the wind began to blow and I grew so cold I was numb. The metal beneath my hands was my lifeline as I explored that silver wall looking for a door.

I never found a door but I found something just as useful. A jagged hole had been torn in the side by the impact and it was large enough for me to crawl through. I entered, carefully avoiding sharp strips of metal and silver splinters that were everywhere. But I got inside.

It was warm. I felt that immediately and breathed a sigh of relief. It would grow colder as time passed but the plane itself would be a place of refuge and I would survive. That was my first thought. I would live.

My second was to wonder what kind of plane it was because it didn't resemble anything I'd ever seen in real life or in pictures. Large and, if I was looking at it correctly, round. Anyway, it looked round, though of course it wasn't because planes aren't round.

I was in a corridor with lights spaced regularly

along the wall that still functioned even after the crash. Both directions were identical so I went to the right because it was as good as the left. I would find the plane's occupants or their bodies.

A sound stopped me. A soft sound. The hair stood up on the back of my neck as I forced myself to look towards that sound because whatever had made it wasn't human. It came from close to the floor so I looked down.

I found myself looking at a tiny calico kitten that was inspecting me with all the interest of a spoiled and very comfortable pet. It came to me, sniffed my pant leg, and then climbed all the way to my shoulder, after which it purred a bit and settled down for a ride.

It took a full minute for me to stop shaking. The kitten had scared me that badly. "Hi, there, little kitten." My voice squeaked. It meowed again, being a conversational kitten. "What's your name?"

It didn't tell me and I still didn't know if the other occupants of the plane were alive but the world changed for the better with that small, warm bundle of fur on my shoulder, so I was able to proceed feeling calmer than since I first saw those storm clouds approach as I tried to change a tire on a car that now was a mangled wreck beneath a pile of rubble that was once part of a mountain.

I walked all around the plane and, yes, it was round because the corridor curved all the way until I once again arrived back at the large, jagged hole I'd climbed through. Except it wasn't large anymore. Myriad multicolored lights flashed on the wall around the hole as something unseen made it grow smaller and still smaller. The kitten and I watched. I'd not be able to enter through that hole now. It was too small.

"What kind of plane repairs itself?" I asked the calico kitten, but it didn't answer. It just purred contentedly and plopped a little lower on my shoulder as it waited for me to take it somewhere. "And where did you come from?" Again, it didn't answer as it looked at me with great interest. "And who do you belong to?" Because obviously it belonged to someone. "And where is your person?"

"Callie?" The kitten jumped from my shoulder and ran towards a male voice that seemed to come from nowhere. "Oh, there you are." The voice was relieved. "Where have you been? I've been looking all over for you."

The voice came closer until a man walked through the inner wall. Just walked through it. He was several years my senior and looking for all the world as normal as possible and he was a bit of a hunk. I noticed that even though I was in shock that he'd just walked through a wall. Or what appeared to be a wall. Obviously, it wasn't one.

Upon seeing me, he stopped short. Grabbed the kitten that jumped onto his shoulder just as it had onto mine, and they both stared at me, the kitten in a friendly way, the man not so much.

"Who are you and what are you doing here?" His voice was forceful and not at all friendly.

I stood my ground. "I could ask you the same thing."

"This is my ship and there's no way you could get inside."

"Yes, there is." I ignored his clearly unfriendly tone and pointed at what remained of the hole, now about the size of a piece of paper surrounded by all those flickering lights that were rapidly repairing it. "I climbed through that hole."

He considered it. "Well, you'll just have to leave because you don't belong here." He grabbed my arm. Hard. "I'll take you to a door since the hole is too small now for you to exit through it."

I shook his arm loose and refused to move. "No!"

That got him. His eyes shot angry sparks. "You don't belong here so you will leave. Or else."

"If I leave, I'll die."

"Huh?"

I couldn't show him the storm raging beyond the plane because there were no windows but I could tell him. "There's a blizzard out there. I'll die if you send me away."

He frowned. "You came from somewhere. Go back to wherever that is."

"I can't." I planted my feet and folded my arms across my chest. "And it's your fault."

"My fault?" His eyes said it couldn't possibly be his fault.

"Your plane crashed into the mountain."

He paused in his efforts to get me to move. "I'll give you that. I did crash."

"The crash caused an avalanche that buried my car and everything I own." The pressure on my arm lessened as those eyes showed the beginning of comprehension. "Your plane caused the problem I'm in now and you can't send me into a blizzard to die. You can't." I could only hope he'd agree that my safety was now his responsibility.

He backed a step and considered me, the kitten on

his shoulder watching the exchange with interest. Eventually he scowled and rubbed the back of his neck with one hand. My dad did that when he didn't know what to do. I hoped that was the case now.

The flickering lights that were repairing the hole went suddenly bright, then zoomed back and forth for a while, then turned a steady blue and stopped flickering. The change meant something to the man, who watched and scowled deeper. "It's too late to do anything now. The hole is repaired enough that we're about to go to the repair shop and there's nothing I can do to stop it. It's on automatic." He stared holes through me. "You're aboard now so you're coming too, whether you want to or not. Whether I want you along or not."

CHAPTER TWO

"REPAIR SHOP?" THAT sounded like civilization. "Good. I want to go there." People. Normalcy. I breathed a sigh of relief that whatever was happening was about to end and I could get back to the life I knew, albeit without a car and everything I needed for college. But there's insurance, I told myself. It would be a hassle, but in the end life would return to normal once we reached that repair shop. "Where's the shop?"

He looked at me and scowled again. "Far away."

"How far?" I put my hands on my hips in my most aggressive manner, something I'm rather good at since I have an older brother.

"Very far." When I waited, he added, "An island."

"Island? We aren't near a lake."

"It's not in a lake. It's in the ocean. Close to Antarctica."

"You're joking." My hands dropped to my side and I forgot to be intimidating.

"I said it was far away and I wish I was joking because now I'm stuck with you until we can get you back where you belong." A rather strong male chin stuck out in what I assumed was meant to be as intimidating as my hands on my hips were meant to be. "We are going half way around the world."

All I could manage was, "Just in case you're telling the truth, how long will it take?"

His brow creased in thought. "Normally half an hour." Sure. Right. A good part of the way around the Earth in half an hour. I'd have laughed if I wasn't in an oddly shaped plane with a strange man and a calico kitten. "With a damaged ship I can't say. Maybe a couple hours. Maybe more. Could be a lot more because we're on reserve power and lucky to have that after what that mountain did to my ship."

"Not to mention what it did to my car. And my life."

"You're alive."

"Thanks to a hole in your plane that no longer exists because this fricking plane repairs itself."

"Enough to get us back to the repair shop. It'll take a long time to get it flyable again."

As we tried to stare each other down, his expression suddenly, inexplicably, softened and his whole demeanor changed.

He gave a huge sigh that said he'd internalized what had happened to me and accepted that I needed help. "I'm glad you're alive. I'm glad there was a hole. I didn't know you were out there. I'd have helped if I'd known." He rubbed the back of his neck again. "So I'm glad the mountain punched a hole in the side of my ship even though it does mean I go to the repair shop instead of where I was headed."

"Was your trip important?" If he was being nice, I would be also and politely inquire as to his plans.

"Nothing that can't be put off until it's repaired."

He'd called his odd craft a ship. Not a plane. "What kind of plane is this, anyway?" I stared at him and dared him to look away. He didn't. He stared at me as hard as I stared at him. "It doesn't seem like the usual kind."

"It's not." We stared at one another some more, eyeball to eyeball, bluff for bluff.

"What kind is it?"

He kind of sagged and decided to stop bluffing and tell me what I wanted to know. "You'd most likely call it a UFO or a UAP. I prefer the old-fashioned term. I call it a flying saucer."

I laughed. I wanted to laugh until tears flowed and I fell on the floor from laughing. But he wasn't laughing. Not even a chuckle. Or a smile. Or anything. So instead of laughing, my stomach did flip-flops as I said, in a squeaky voice, "You're not kidding."

He shook his head. "Nope. You're in a flying saucer."

I wanted to run. Hide. Get away from whatever was happening because this was definitely abnormal and I was in the middle of it and, now that I thought about it, there were hieroglyphics on the walls that didn't resemble anything I'd ever seen in history books or elsewhere and I'd heard that flying saucers had hieroglyphics.

He waited until I accepted that I was inside a flying saucer. Then he turned and led the way through that wall that turned not to be a solid wall after all. Rather it was a wall with a doorway that was a hologram, and you'd only know where it was if you knew the entirety of the ship. I'd have been stuck in the outer hall forever without his guidance.

We ended up in what was clearly a control room above the main body of the craft, with windows all around and flickering lights everywhere and comfortable seats near the center with a control panel close by.

I could see out the windows. We'd already gone above the storm. Now we passed through more clouds and then we rose above them, too, and then there was only empty sky through which we moved silently. Too silently. It was creepy. The whole thing was creepy. "What happens to me when we reach Antarctica?" If that was truly where we were headed.

"We'll figure that out when we get there."

I'd read stories. Watched movies. I knew the drill. "Will I be killed because I'm going to see stuff I shouldn't?"

"I doubt it." He didn't say for sure, just that he doubted I'd die. "We don't work that way." But there was the tiniest uncertainty in his voice.

I tried to keep my voice from wavering. "Who is this 'we' that'll decide my fate?"

He sighed. "You ask too many questions, and I can't answer any of them so I suggest you enjoy the ride because you're on your way to an island near Antarctica whether you wish it or not."

At that moment the kitten jumped down from his shoulder and started to wander around the room that had kitten food and water and a litter box in one corner next to quite strange controls except it wasn't truly a corner because it was a round room, which figured, being in the center of a round flying saucer.

The kitten was well cared for, which meant this man cared about his kitten. I could only hope that concern for life extended to me. I told myself to forget about that tiny hesitation when he said I wouldn't be killed and to do what he suggested. I looked him up and down and said, "I doubt I'll enjoy myself."

He sighed, accepting my answer. "I'm Jack Rutherford," he said simply.

"<u>Elena</u> Elder." Then there was nothing more to say and we each found things to do that enabled us to ignore each other. For a while.

But it was soon clear that the trip was taking longer than expected, something I figured from Jack's expression and the way he stared into the control panel. And the way he frowned. "The damage must be significant or we'd have been there by now."

He checked what must be gauges on the control panel by his chair, then he muttered and paced the floor. Then he did those things all over again. Back and forth, back and forth. "Communication is out so I can't tell anyone what's going on."

"Do you still think we'll be there in a couple hours?"

He stopped pacing and calculated mentally because the ship – flying saucer – evidently wasn't up to doing it for him in its current crippled state. I was pretty sure it normally did such things. It was a flying saucer, after all. It was a weird, science fiction thing and everyone knew they could do anything. "Longer than a couple hours. Maybe a day."

His voice said that was slow as molasses compared to his usual speed. "I hope just one day." He stopped pacing long enough to consider our circumstances. "I hope it doesn't take longer or the entire world will notice us and come with guns blazing." He glanced out the windows. "And we're losing altitude fast, which makes being sighted more likely."

"Will we crash?" The flying saucer had already crashed once and was crippled.

"The loss of altitude isn't drastic, just a way of conserving power because we can ride the atmosphere somewhat, but we are dropping low enough to be seen."

"Will someone really come after us?"

"They usually do."

After that we stopped talking. We developed a routine. He stared at me or I stared at him until whoever was doing the staring would realize they were staring and abruptly look away. It got to be annoying. It also was interesting.

I didn't know what he saw when he looked at me. A smallish coed with longish, brown hair who was absolutely average in every way. Nothing spectacular and I was without makeup and wearing old jeans and a light jacket. When I looked at him, I saw a six foot something piece of rather better than average male flesh who didn't seem to know he was a hunk wearing equally old jeans that fit him a lot better than mine fit me.

He didn't seem to know he was a hunk. I'd not met any good-looking male before who didn't know exactly how attractive he was. Why didn't this Jack Rutherford know? More to the point, what exactly did he do that he didn't seem to know anything about himself in relation to other people? Was he a hermit? Did his unusual job isolate him from human contact? Was he absorbed in his flying saucer to the extent of not seeing anything else? I decided the answer to all those questions was 'maybe.'

And what about this flying saucer? Did it belong to him or was he an employee of some weird business? Maybe a black, government op? I finally decided to end our staring at each other before one of us snapped. "Mind if I check out this craft?" I couldn't bring myself to call it a flying saucer because everyone knows there is no such thing.

"Help yourself." So, I wandered through that holographic doorway to investigate. If I looked carefully, I could see where the doorway differed subtly from the wall. I figured Jack was glad to have me out of his sight.

I discovered cots for napping, a larder filled with enough food for a few days, a couple comfortable chairs, cat stuff, a small bathroom, a half-finished novel, and not much more. Enough to know the flying saucer could hold people and a kitten but it wasn't outfitted for long journeys.

"I have a question," I said when I once more returned to the control room. Jack turned toward me, and I wished I knew how to diplomatically ask. But I didn't. "Um – are you – um – human?"

His answer was an immediate loud bark of laughter. "I was born in Kansas so I know some New Yorkers who'd say I'm not. But I consider myself human." I colored and left the control room to inspect his craft a second time in order to avoid having to face that spontaneous laugh. The laugh said that of course he was human. But I felt justified in wondering if he was something else.

I eventually figured enough time had passed that he'd stopped laughing so I returned to the control room. Jack was in the command chair when I walked through that holographic door to find him examining the panel before him as if the blinking lights meant something. Callie ran to me, and I put her on my shoulder where she purred and the two of us headed for the windows to see what we could see, ignoring Jack completely. I figured the view might be spectacular.

I looked out the windows and almost puked. Two fighter jets with flags on the sides that I didn't recognize were heading our way.

CHAPTER THREE

"ARE THEY GOING to shoot?"

"Probably."

"Will they destroy us?"

"Of course not."

"They look pretty deadly to me."

"We're in a bubble. It's like a universe within a universe. Nothing can penetrate the bubble."

"You crashed into a mountain and we're on reserve power."

"So we did and that crash damaged the bubble and we're growing weaker by the hour. But the bubble still exists and when I saw the jets, I diverted more power to the bubble."

"But we can still fly?"

"Barely."

What he said wasn't all that reassuring. "Are you sure they can't hurt us?"

He gave a patient sigh and rose from the chair to join me at the window. "Watch. See for yourself."

I looked from him to the fighter jets and then back to the control panel. "Shouldn't you be doing something? Flying this thing? Taking care of business? Doing something to keep us alive?"

"Not necessary. Besides, like I believe I already told you, once the saucer crashed, automation took over. There's not much I can do now and nothing I need to do. But don't worry, we're safe. I was just checking to see how much longer before we reach the repair shop." He looked down at me. "Because you wanted to know."

He watched the jets with interest but there wasn't a hint of fear in that look. I tried to match what was obviously a belief in our invincibility and pretty much failed because as we watched, the covers to what must be rockets came off and were aimed at us.

"They're going to shoot."

"Yep." Still no fear.

I gulped. He turned at the sound. Sighed. Pulled me close and wrapped an arm around me as if I was a toddler in need of comfort, which was pretty much what I felt like. Instead of pushing him away in distain I leaned into what turned out to be a hard, masculine body and greedily grabbed every crumb of comfort he was willing to share as he repeated what he'd said before. "Watch this. It'll be interesting."

Projectiles came at us. Hit the window we were looking through. Exploded. I ducked, winced, and almost crawled into Jack. He sighed again and pulled me still closer if such was possible, which it wasn't because a piece of paper wouldn't fit between us. I felt his eyes on me as mine were glued to the flash of light mere feet from where we stood. But that flash remained outside the window. Inside nothing changed and we felt nothing. Absolutely nothing. Callie the kitten didn't even look up.

I was stunned and relieved. "We're safe."

With effort he kept his voice from expressing the condescension he was clearly feeling. "As I said we would be."

I pulled an inch or so away and straightened my clothes that had been mashed against him. "Those jets looked so lethal."

"They are lethal, just not to this baby." He'd have patted his flying saucer if his hands weren't full of me. Even as I pulled away his eyes, that I finally noticed were blue, remained on me instead of the jets that were trying to kill us. But he saw them from the corner of his eye.

"Uh oh," he said suddenly, moving his eyes away from me and towards the jets. "Does that pilot have a death wish?"

One of the jets was heading straight for us. We could see the pilot's eyes and the look on his face that said he was going to ram us if it was the last thing he did. I gasped and Jack forgot me as he ran for that command chair.

His fingers danced over the brightly colored board in front of him and suddenly we weren't where we'd been mini-seconds before. The jet flew safely through the space we no longer occupied, and I found myself turning to another window on the opposite side of the saucer as Jack returned and examined me to see if I still needed comfort. "It just kept flying," I said, unable to keep wonderment out of my voice.

"That was close." His voice showed emotion . He cared about the pilot. "He could have died. Idiot."

"You saved him, didn't you?" I turned towards him accusingly and stared into his eyes, a space of a foot or less. "This thing wouldn't have moved if you hadn't done something even though you said it was on automatic. That jet would be in pieces."

If I wasn't so close, I'd not have seen the relief in his face. "That would have been the end of the jet and its pilot, and I could only do something because it was so close. I could maneuver a bit."

"Why didn't he know we meant no harm? Surely, he saw we weren't the military. No uniforms."

"He couldn't see us. It's another thing about this baby. We can see out but he can't see in."

"Would the collision have damaged this craft? This flying saucer?"

"Of course not."

"Then why did hitting a mountain damage it if a collision with a jet wouldn't?"

I saw the uncertainty in his eyes only because we were once again close. "That's the million-dollar question, though a mountain is substantially more than a mere jet." His lips thinned. "I hope we'll know when it's run through diagnostics."

Those blue eyes dropped to my face. He didn't try to hide his concern. "Because it shouldn't have happened. This baby should have gone over the mountain without any problem. But it didn't." He put me inches away from his body and the air between us was unexpectedly cool but he hadn't pushed me far enough away that I could no longer read his thoughts, just far enough for him to be able to also read mine. "If things had happened correctly, I'd be somewhere else, and you'd be on your way to wherever you were going."

"Or freezing to death in a useless car in a blizzard." Then I added impulsively, without knowing where the words or the thought came from, only that I meant them. "I'm glad it happened because I'm here and warm and comfortable." I thought over what I'd just said. "I will be glad provided I get out of this alive."

He laughed. The sound was honest, unlike his first hard laugh, and came from deep inside of him. "You will. Alive, healthy, and with your memory intact. I promise." He meant it and I wondered what had changed him from the scowling, insulting male who wanted to send me packing into a decent, possibly nice human, though I mentally emphasized the 'possibly' because I wasn't out of this predicament yet.

"You are a small thing, aren't you?" His voice was full of amusement. So maybe my size decided him I wasn't a threat. If so, good for me and good for my future release from wherever we were going.

We remained at the window until the jets gave up their pursuit and disappeared. "What will they tell their superiors?"

"An interesting story that'll probably be all over the world by this evening."

"And no one will believe it."

He rubbed the back of his neck. "I hope not."

All that potential publicity bothered him. "You people depend on no one believing you exist, don't you?" His softer demeanor emboldened me to ask what I'd not have asked earlier.

Another neck rub. He dropped his hand when he saw I'd noticed. But his answer, like the one earlier, was honest. "Life is much simpler when we are relegated to the back pages along with the Loch Ness monster and Elvis sightings."

After that, he returned to that centrally located chair with a control panel while I went back to going from one window to the next to stare at a sky that didn't change and was fascinating anyway. It was a beautiful blue sky, and we were in the middle of it without sound or any sense of motion. I could have been in my parents' house on its rock-solid concrete foundation instead of flying through the sky at incredible speed even though that speed was slow compared to what it could go.

I decided we were going straight south because Antarctica was south though the earth was so far below it was impossible to make out land formations or continents. All I could do was wait and wonder if Jack's estimate of our arrival was right. I watched day fade into twilight and then watched as the sun set before we dropped out of the sky. It was dark and the clouds we flew through had been so far below us that seeing them was the only way I knew we were about to land.

A continent appeared beneath us, ghost-like white in the dark of night. Antarctica. But we didn't head there. Instead, we sought out a tiny island that was merely a dot until we were close. Then I barely made out a mountain sticking out of the Antarctic Ocean. No beach, there was just snow-covered mountain and ocean.

I looked for a landing field. I saw nothing. As we dropped, we headed straight for the icy ocean. I found myself instinctively ducking as we approached the water. Then we dove straight into the ocean and dark water took the place of the night sky beyond the windows.

CHAPTER FOUR

The saucer must have slowed but there was no matching sensation. As far as I could tell, it simply went from full speed to stop in less than a second without me feeling a thing as we glided through water and then above it into a cave and stopped. A door I'd not realized existed opened and a ramp slid down so we could disembark.

Jack picked up Callie and took me by the arm. "We're home." I noted the way he said it. Home. With all the emotions the word implied. "Let's get you introduced."

My insides turned to ice as I marched with Jack down that ramp and towards a somewhat elderly man with graying hair who was wearing an old, comfortable sweater with holes in the elbows. He was coming to meet us. Halfway to us, he caught sight of me.

He stopped. Froze in place. Examined me, top to bottom along with the fact that Jack was holding me. He must have decided I didn't pose a threat since I was immobilized by Jack's arm so he continued on towards us but now his focus was entirely on me. "I see we have a guest," he said in a totally neutral voice when he was close enough to be heard.

"Thom, this is <u>Elena</u> Elder."

More inspection. "So, I see." He came close and shook my hand. "How do you do, <u>Elena</u> Elder." Still with no expression as he waited for the explanation he was sure would come.

"Elena, meet Thom Atlas." Then he added, "And welcome to the Atlas Project." Jack explained briefly why I was there, including that the flying saucer needed repairs. Thom nodded. "I wondered why I didn't hear from you. I'm glad you made it back." A slight tremor in his voice said he'd been concerned.

He went to the flying saucer and walked around it much as I'd done in the snowstorm, touching it now and then, nodding as he found irregularities in its side that I couldn't see. "We'll get this thing hooked up to diagnostics and see what's going on." His eyebrows came together. "And find out why she rammed a mountain instead of going over it."

"What about <u>Elena</u>?" Jack pulled Thom's attention away from the saucer.

Thom set the inner workings of flying saucers aside in order to examine me more thoroughly. "You're young." Like that was a crime. "Are your parents looking for you?"

I explained that I'd been on my way to summer school at the college I attended and had given myself a week in order to do some sightseeing on the way. "So, no search parties are likely looking for you? At least not yet?" I said I didn't think so. He nodded shortly. "Good. That gives us time to come up with a plan."

"But my car and everything I own are now beneath a pile of dirt."

"Things are replaceable. It's you we must figure how to deal with, and we have a week to do so." He turned to Jack. "Find a room for her and clothes and whatever else she needs."

Then Thom turned back to the flying saucer that was his first concern. But before he forgot the world completely in order to deal with what was obviously his first love, he turned towards the door he'd come through as a full-grown gray and white cat came through and meandered towards him, followed by two kittens. Mother and three kittens, I decided, one of which rode Jack's shoulder.

Jack noticed my interest. "Thom likes cats and his cat had kittens. I ended up with Callie. They do make the place a little less stark."

I soon learned that the place, as he called it, was huge and, yes, it was stark. He led me towards my future accommodations. Because I was going to stay long enough to need them. A problem? I hoped not.

We went along main corridors with smaller ones branching off that led to places I couldn't see. The whole thing had a military feel to it. We seemed to walk forever, and I figured it must fill the entire inside of the island including the mountain I'd seen from the air because there were elevators now and then that must lead to additional levels.

We took an elevator to a higher floor and still all the corridors were empty. I wanted to ask where the people were but I'd already decided not to ask too many questions because I didn't want to know so much that they wouldn't let me leave.

Jack showed me a room with a bath. "This is for you." He pointed to the hall floor. "Follow the red arrows to the dining room when you're hungry." Then he pointed to the lower half of the walls of the corridor that were also painted a bright red. "Red is for living quarters and everything involved with everyday life. Eating. Exercising. Recreation. And so forth." Then he added, "Arrows always point to elevators except on the living floor. Here they point to the kitchen. But the elevators here are near the kitchen so in a way they do point to elevators on this floor also."

Yellow, it seemed, was for offices and blue for anything that involved the flying saucers themselves. Maintenance. Parking. He informed me that there was a lot of blue. Green was for everything else.

"We don't have set mealtimes and there's no cook, just what we make ourselves, but there are vending machines and stuff in the refrigerators and freezers if you're willing to cook."

Then he smacked his forehead. "I forgot clothes. Sorry." So instead of leaving me in what was now my room we went down several red hallways to a cavernous room filled with boxes of all sizes and shapes. "There should be something here that'll fit." He scowled. "We have everything imaginable here including clothes of all sizes." We checked labels on dozens of boxes until we found where clothes were located and then, sure enough, there were several pairs of sweats that fit and shirts that were too big but wearable, along with everything else I could need. "These will have to do for now."

"I can pay when I get home and get a check from the insurance company."

"Not necessary."

He grabbed my new wardrobe and led me back to

my room. I realized I must be getting the layout of the place because I didn't need him to show me where it was, thanks to the color-coding system. Before shutting the door, he reminded me to follow the red arrows when I was hungry and said he'd see me later, though he wasn't specific as to when that would be. Then I was alone.

I dropped into a comfortable chair and put my head in my hands. Had I truly been on my way to college just that morning? So much had happened that it seemed like ages had passed since then. I felt a need to do something. To come to grips with what had happened and where I was. To feel normal.

A long, hot shower helped clear my mind but when I was dry and dressed in new sweats and a too-large shirt, I paced the floor like a caged animal and though it was a reasonably sized room, no room was large enough for me to shed the nervous energy that held me in thrall. I crawled into the comfortable bed and tried to sleep but that didn't happen either.

I was in a super-secret facility inside of an Antarctic island that held flying saucers and the people who flew and repaired them. Who could sleep? Not me. So I gave up and went in search of the kitchen. Maybe they had hot cocoa and sleeping pills.

Follow the red arrows, he'd said. I did so and found myself in a largish room with tables with what looked like a commercial kitchen to one side. There were vending machines on the opposite wall. I had no money to use them so I was about to head for the kitchen when I heard a voice. "The vending machines work without money" Jack walked into the room. "We jimmied them when we ran out of quarters."

He came close and we stood staring at each other. Face to face. Until he said, "I couldn't sleep either." He rubbed the back of his neck. "I can't stop wondering why the saucer flew into a mountain. I play those few seconds over and over in my head."

He shook his head to get rid of demons and led me to the kitchen. "I was thinking of cooking dinner. Take my mind off recalcitrant saucers. How about we work together and cook up a meal?"

"What about Thom?"

"We'll make extra." He opened a couple cabinets and a refrigerator. The insides held much the same ingredients as my mother's kitchen so soon we were chopping and stirring and tasting spaghetti sauce while waiting for noodles to finish cooking and garlic bread to toast.

I surprised myself by being hungry. I decided that might be a good thing. Maybe with something in my stomach I'd be able to sleep when I returned to my room. Which brought up a question. Time. "What time is it?" Was it time to sleep or too early to turn in?

He tipped his head towards a clock on the wall that I'd not noticed. "You'll get a cell phone to replace the one you lost when your car was buried, and you'll know the time from it." He looked at me thoughtfully. "But I don't think that'll happen until Thom is comfortable that you won't call friends and tell them about this place. So, it might be a while. In the meantime, the kitchen isn't the only place with a clock. Clocks being the only way to tell time here because there are no windows."

We strained the noodles and filled our plates. "You said your family isn't looking for you."

"I doubt they know anything happened but since I can't communicate, I can't know that for sure. A cell phone would be nice."

"I'll get you one as soon as Thom okays it." As soon as I was deemed to not be a threat.

When we finished, we cleaned up together and put the uneaten spaghetti in a bowl with a note for Thom. It was a normal thing to do and I felt myself relaxing. Mostly, though, I was oddly comfortable working beside Jack. Like a guest instead of a prisoner though I was pretty sure that if I tried to go where I shouldn't, I'd quickly learn that this place could be a kind of prison.

I didn't want to return to my room until I was exhausted. Then maybe I'd sleep. "Is there anything to do around here?"

At that moment, Thom entered the kitchen, sniffed, went straight to the refrigerator, took out the spaghetti and popped it in a microwave. Jack got him some dinnerware. As they took everything to a table, he spoke to Thom so quietly that I couldn't understand a word. Thom nodded briefly and replied just as quietly. Then Jack left Thom to his dinner and returned to me.

"There's a library and tomorrow Thom says I should give you the grand tour." His tone of voice said he hadn't expected Thom to let me see much of the facility. Later, in what turned out to be a well-stocked library, he said more. "Thom put me in charge of you while you're here." After a momentary hesitation, he added, "He even said no place is off limits. You can wander wherever you wish."

"Because I'm never going to leave so it doesn't matter what I see?"

He laughed. Then he laughed some more. A normal laugh. "Thom reminded me that if you tell someone what you see they won't believe you so there's no reason to restrict your movements." The laughter remained in those blue eyes. "When it's light out, we can even go outside. The view is spectacular."

"This is Antarctica. Isn't it cold outside?"

"Very. But we have parkas."

I found a couple books that I brought back to my room and tried to read but all they did was put me to sleep. Which, when I thought about it, was exactly what I needed and when I awoke the next morning and showered and climbed into a clean pair of sweats, I felt refreshed.

I put my room in order and went in search of breakfast, figuring I was most likely to find Jack in the kitchen. No use looking for him elsewhere because he hadn't said where his room was located. I decided to ask how to get hold of him if I needed something, realizing I'd given up on my decision not to ask questions. Because I had a million.

CHAPTER FIVE

Jack was already in the kitchen. "You like bacon and eggs?" When I didn't answer, he said, "Anything else you have to fix yourself but I'm already making bacon and eggs." He dropped several slices of bacon into a frying pan. Just like at home. Just like normal. As if this was a normal day in a normal place. Which it probably was to him.

"Whatever you're having is fine." Still no people. We were the only ones in the kitchen. The only people anywhere as far as I could tell, except for Thom who appeared and disappeared on some unknown schedule. "Has everyone else eaten?" A way of finding out if this huge place housed only two people and one incidental visitor. Me.

He placed the frying pan carefully on the burner and gave me a long, slow look. He knew what I was asking. "We three are all the people around at the moment." Which told me nothing at all.

"Thom seems nice," I said later as a way of starting a conversation as I picked at excellent scrambled eggs.

Again, Jack knew what I was doing. "Yes, he is." Such a long silence stretched after his few words that eventually he added, as a nod to my attempt at conversation. "He's also the owner of this place. Which is why it's called the Atlas Project. Because his last name is Atlas."

"He doesn't seem like the owner of an entire island."

"Two islands, actually. The other one is in the Bahamas, plus he has a ranch in the mountains of the western USA, though those places aren't as large as this one."

I blurted out, "Is that where everyone else is?"

"Families pretty much stay on the island in the Bahamas. But it's spring now so people like to visit families and celebrate Easter. The rest, those who are still around, are most likely on patrol."

"On patrol?" Now we were getting someplace. "What do you patrol?"

His head tipped and his eyes shone with appreciation for my sidewise quest for information. "You're a nosy little thing, aren't you?"

"Just making conversation." This little game we were playing was going nowhere. "I'm curious about this place, that's all. Thom doesn't seem to mind if I know what it's about."

He was done with his breakfast while I was just starting. He poured himself another cup of coffee and returned to wait for me to finish. I started actually eating because he clearly wasn't leaving until I was done. "Want the short version or the long one?"

"Whichever you feel like."

"Then here goes. The semi short version. Jack is a mechanical engineer. A genius. About thirty or so years ago he ended up in a flying saucer in much the same way you did. A crash that he investigated and, like you, he ended up here. Being a mechanical genius, he stuck around and figured out how they work, and the rest is history."

"So, he didn't make them?"

"No one knows who made them. We do know that whoever it was is long gone."

"But Thom figured how to fly them?"

"He did because he's a genius, and after that, since they go through water as well as air, he used them to scoop up treasure from the ocean floor that pays for everything you are enjoying."

"He built this place?"

Jack shook his head. "It was already here. The treasure financed making it suitable for us."

"Who was here before you? Human beings?" In a corner of my mind, I thought how quickly I'd got to asking questions that a week ago would have been insane.

"We think humans built the saucers because they and everything about this place fits us perfectly but we've never seen any of them or pictures of them so we don't know for sure. We don't even know how long ago this place was built. We think thousands of years ago. Or more."

I struggled to take in what he was saying. "No major changes were needed, just fixing the place so we can live and work in comfort." A sweep of an arm took in the kitchen and the tables where we sat. "It's as close to a home as a dedicated bachelor could design."

"Accept it's in an island in the Antarctic Ocean and the only way in or out is through water."

"You get used to it."

"And now he knows everything about flying saucers? I'm surprised you call them flying saucers. Why not UFOs or UAPs? Those are the latest names for them."

"Because that's what they were called when I discovered this place and is what we still call them. Saucers for short." A voice from behind us broke in. "And no, I do not know everything." Thom checked out our breakfast and headed for the kitchen to whip up something for himself. "I've barely scratched the surface of what these flying gizmos can do. The technology is way beyond anything we have now." He poured himself a bowl of cold cereal with milk and brought it to our table. "What happened to you is an example of what I don't know, though I believe I've cracked that particular mystery and added to a growing stash of information about saucers in the process."

Jack leaned forward. "You know why it crashed?"

Thom nodded. "I do indeed." He started at his cereal, brandishing the spoon like a baton. "It seems our military is experimenting with microwaves and at the very moment and in the exact place where you crashed, two microwave beams – intended for military use, I'm sure – met each other and kind of exploded and you were in the wrong place at the wrong time."

Jack leaned back in his chair. "So microwaves caused the crash. Can we prevent it happening again in case microwave weaponry becomes commonplace?"

"I've adjusted the sensors to pick up their frequency so it'll never happen again. It'll take a while to reprogram all the saucers, of course, but no one will ever again have to go through what you did." He turned to me. "Or you, Miss Elder, and I'm sorry for what happened to your car and your belongings."

Then he forgot I existed as he rose, took his dirty dishes to the kitchen and returned to wherever he came from. "He's going to contact everyone on patrol and warn them to watch where they're going until he can reprogram all the saucers." Jack knew his boss.

Something Thom had said made no sense. "Why didn't he know the military was using microwaves?"

"Why should he know what they were doing?"

I indicated the room we were in. The entire facility. The island. "Isn't this a government project? I know he discovered the flying saucers but surely, he told the government about them and they are now in charge."

"No!" It wasn't a statement. He shouted.

"Why not?"

Jack glowered. "If a government – any government – got hold of this technology, think what those in power would do. It would be World War III. I pray that never, ever happens." His eyes held mine. "And don't even think of telling anyone about this place when you leave."

I shrank under that glower. "Okay. I won't say a word." But there was still a question to be answered. "Thom doesn't know everything about the saucers. He said so, that he's just scratched the surface. Doesn't that bother you?"

"I trust the saucers and I trust Thom. The crash that brought you here was an anomaly." Jack gathered our dishes and headed for the kitchen. He was possibly a bit huffy. "Besides, I knew what I was signing up for when I took this job. I knew there'd be risk and I accepted the possibility." He deposited dirty dishes in a dishwasher and returned. "Now, according to Thom, I'm in charge of you. Do you want that tour?"

I soon learned that there were more levels than I could count, all connected by elevators. On every level the bottom half of the halls were painted red or blue or green or yellow with doors with signs on them that said what they were for and who worked in them but none were occupied that I could see and the rooms seemed to go on forever. "This place is huge."

"Larger than what we need but it's what was here when Thom arrived."

"I didn't see any buildings when we came. Just ice and snow on a mountain."

"You won't see any because this facility is inside the mountain instead of on it. But there's a viewing room at the top with windows in all directions and you can go outside from there if you want."

"It's cold."

"There are parkas and everything you need. Remember? Everyone goes out at least once when they first arrive because it's such a unique experience. After that, not so much."

"I want to go outside." I remembered the blizzard that had blanketed the world when the saucer crashed. "If the weather's decent. I've had enough of blizzards for a while."

"Let's find out."

He took my hand and pulled me towards still another bank of elevators. Callie followed and climbed to Jack's shoulder from where she stared at me as if I might be her next ride. Soon we were at the highest point of the facility. The top of the mountain. It was a small mountain, actually, perhaps only a high hill, but it was the entirety of the island, so it seemed huge.

We exited that elevator into a room with windows all around and Jack was right, the view was spectacular. I stared and forgot about everything except the blue ocean and white world beyond those windows. There was a starkness about it that held me silent for a long time. Then I turned to Jack. "I want to go outside." Because it was beautiful as well as deadly.

There was a closet of sorts in the center of the room filled with parkas, snowpants, boots, mittens and everything needed for an assault on the cold. We dressed warmly and headed for the single door that led to a balcony. Jack made sure Callie stayed inside.

Even wearing warm clothing, the blast of cold air almost stopped me in my tracks. The late spring blizzard back home was nothing compared to the bitter, breath-stealing cold that was the Antarctic. We carefully, one step at a time, went down ice-covered stairs to an observation deck suspended over the Antarctic Ocean that gave the appearance of an ice shelf. No one not from the facility would know it was man-made. From there we watched waves break against the icy shore for a long time. I could have stayed there forever, watching those waves.

After a few minutes, though, Jack signaled it was time to return to the warmth of the viewing room and he was right, the cold was beginning to penetrate even the warm clothing we wore. It took longer to remove all those outer garments than it had to put them on because in the short time we'd been outside they'd accumulated a layer of ice that thawed in the warm room and trickled onto the floor.

We hung up everything on racks to let them thaw

and went once more to the windows to look where we'd just been. I found myself looking sidewise at Jack more than at the landscape. What kind of man voluntarily came to a place like this to work and live? He'd been a scowling threat to my safety when I first met him. Now he was an interesting enigma.

"Want to go out again?" Jack knew what my answer would be. That smile I'd come to recognize as specific to him flashed as he turned from the icy world beyond the window to me and back again.

"You're an ice princess." He turned me towards a mirror. My nose was red. His smile broadened and I found myself laughing too.

"I'm not going back outside for a long time. Maybe never." I shivered. "I'm amazed this place is so warm. It's like summer inside. The technology must be amazing."

"The technology feels alien though everything seems to have been designed for humans."

"So, you don't have a clue about the builders?"

"Neither who nor when." Jack's hands remained on my shoulders from turning me towards the mirror. Our gazes met in the reflection. Two humans merged into one in the shiny surface. "Was that mirror always there?" He didn't know. "Do you suppose it reflected aliens long ago? Or were they human beings?" He didn't know that, either.

Which brought up another question. I was full of them. They crowded my mind. "You haven't run across any other humans or other beings on your patrols?"

"Nope."

"People see flying saucers all the time. Are all of them from here?"

"Yep."

"There are so many sightings. Hundreds. Thousands."

"Most are hallucinations. A very few are genuine. The thing is, the flying saucers Thom found were autonomously following a program created long before any of us was born and he's still working on disabling that program because now there are people who can fly them so they don't have to fly themselves. Not all the saucers are autonomous, though. The ones we use require a pilot but others still follow a schedule we don't yet understand. So, there are flying saucers out there all the time."

"They are ghost crafts."

"You're right about that. It's why we refer to ourselves as ghosts. Because that's kind of what we are." He hesitated, then continued, "It started as a joke and the name stuck because as far as the world is concerned, we don't exist. We are ghosts."

"You say 'we,' but I haven't seen anyone besides you and Thom."

"If you stay long enough, you'll meet the rest." He said it in such an odd voice that I was certain the other inhabitants of the island were staying away deliberately. They were making sure I didn't see them. So, I'd not be able to identify them?

In the elevator on the way back to our living quarters with Callie riding my shoulder and watching Jack, I asked another question, one that came from the way that vast, white world affected me. I'd felt an odd tug from the stark whiteness beyond the windows that led to me asking a philosophical type question. "Why are you doing this? Why live in this remote corner of the world? Why did Thom create this company?"

"For the betterment of mankind." Jack flushed but didn't look away. "I know it sounds foolish and naive but Thom truly believes that if some of us are already out there in the solar system when the rest of mankind arrives, there'll be less chance of any nasty confrontation that will end in Armageddon. And since we'll already have what those newcomers will be looking for it'll be in their best interests to make peace with us instead of trying to take us or each other out."

"The solar system? You patrol the entire solar system? Not just Earth?"

"The entire solar system. We could go farther if we choose but so far we haven't."

"Could those newcomers you mention who will reach space someday take you out when they develop spaceships and find you are already where they want to be and already own the things they want?"

"Not a chance." He spoke with a calm conviction that said he knew things about the saucers that I didn't. That conviction made me a believer, that and the memory of the jets that failed to take us out while we were on our way here.

The remainder of the elevator ride was silent. The entire facility was so huge and so strange I decided I'd had enough for one day and spent the afternoon in the library reading about flying saucers. I quickly realized I knew more about the mysterious craft than any of the authors and I'd only been at the facility for a day.

CHAPTER SIX

I WAS ON my own the next day, alone in the kitchen until Thom arrived. He explained. "I needed Jack to take a saucer on a test flight."

"The one that crashed? Is it repaired?"

"Not that one. A different one I've been working on. I think I have the autonomous flight controller deactivated but I want to make sure. I asked him to take it out for a run and see if it goes where he wants it to go instead of where it was programmed to go thousands of years ago."

"What if the deactivation doesn't work?"

Thom's eyes rolled. "Then he'll be gone for a long time, and I'll have to take you home." He looked at me oddly. "Jack wants to take you. Don't know why. Feels responsible, maybe. But no matter what happens, he'll be back eventually. The saucers always come back, and we made sure this one is stocked for a long trip should that be what happens." He noticed my doubt. "You came here in one of the smaller saucers. Jack is testing a really big one that was designed for long voyages."

I didn't ask how big or what duration the trip would involve or where that voyage might take Jack. But the conversation made me wonder. If the saucer I'd ridden was small, how large, exactly, was a really big one?

I left the kitchen considering what to do with a day to myself but the question about flying saucer size was ticking my brain and I couldn't push it away. I had the run of the facility thanks to the no-one-will-believe-you scenario so I could go anywhere. Everywhere. Even wherever the saucers were parked.

I felt a growing thread of excitement as I realized I could find those large saucers and uncover the reality of these strange craft that disbelievers said were hallucinations that I now knew were real. And no one would stop me because I could go anywhere.

How to go about finding them? First, I decided, I should spend some time checking out places we'd passed the day before and look them over closer because revisiting them was what I was pretty sure Thom expected me to do. But the facility seemed pretty similar to any large office building in any city on Earth only without windows. Nothing special about it other than it was inside a mountain in Antarctica.

After giving the familiar rooms a cursory examination, though, I'd go looking for flying saucers. They had to be somewhere and if I looked hard enough, I'd find a flying saucer hanger. I wished I had a cell phone to take pictures. But of course, I didn't because they didn't want me taking pictures.

I entered the nearest elevator to go to the observation room because the view was spectacular and because I should be returning there like a good tourist. I reached out to push the 'up' button. Then I hesitated and, instead of going up, I pushed the 'down' button because a saucer hanger would most likely be at the lowest level. Near the ocean.

I wouldn't check out the facility a second time after all. I'd already seen the observation room and the kitchen and a few other places and didn't need a refresher. Besides, even though I'd seen the saucer I arrived in, they'd never be boring. And this could be my only chance and I didn't want to squander what might be limited free time visiting places I already knew. So, I pushed the 'down' button.

When I stepped out of the elevator on the lowest level, the walls were yellow. Offices. Not what I wanted but that was what stared back at me.

Then I started thinking. Perhaps they were offices for the people who flew saucers. If so, they'd most likely be close to the launch area and that meant I was in the right general area. I just had to find blue arrows. Blue for saucers.

I checked a few office doors. None were locked. Because they were empty or because nothing was secret? I entered one that was empty and a couple with desks and computers that were turned off but plugged into outlets. Those offices had papers scattered about. So some of the offices were used and I figured I must be headed in the right direction.

Eventually I rounded a corner and the walls changed to blue. Blue for saucers. I checked the direction of those blue arrows. They all pointed the same way, which would be to the elevators. So, I went in the opposite direction. I'd backtrack the arrows and eventually find the saucer hanger because I figured people would normally head for the elevator when they finished a patrol to get to their living quarters. So, the saucers would be in the opposite direction.

It was a good plan and it worked.

I reached a door just like all the other doors but when I pushed this one open, I found myself on a platform overlooking flying saucers. Hundreds of them. The hanger went on forever filling more space than I'd thought the entire facility included so this place must be under water.

They were awesome, sitting in silent majesty in the stillness of that vast space. Some were so large they made the one I'd been in look like a puddle jumper by comparison and all were in rows according to size starting with the smallest ones nearest the platform I was on and growing larger until the largest, the behemoths, ranged along the far side. I didn't even try to count them.

Every one of them shone silver in the dim light and appeared ready to fly on a moment's notice. I shivered from excitement because I was in the hanger. I'd found it. I could walk among flying saucers.

I descended the stairs and found myself beside one similar to the one I'd been in. I walked all around it, touching the silver side while remembering the walk I'd taken around one just like it in a blizzard. Then I looked farther afield to decide where to go next.

I stopped abruptly. My skin crawled. In the minutes since descending the stairs, something had changed. Something was happening.

I could feel it but there was no sound, no vibration, nothing except a feeling that something was happening that grew stronger the longer I stood there trying to locate its origin. I decided the best thing was to leave. I returned to the platform to leave the hanger. I climbed the stairs to the platform. I was about to leave the hanger when something on the far side of the hanger caught my attention.

Lights flashed where the largest of the saucers were parked. There was no sound but many colored lights flickered and moved in a pattern I recognized. It was similar to how the lights in the saucer had flashed while repairing the hole in its side. They were doing something. But what?

I leaned over the railing and stared but couldn't make out what was happening so far away. I wanted to know and the fact that something was happening made the wanting sharper.

This could be my only chance ever to see a flying saucer in action and whatever was happening involved some kind of action. If I was closer, I'd see what was going on and it was surely something I'd remember for the rest of my life. I couldn't pass up the opportunity. I wouldn't.

I ran down those stairs double time and across the hanger, dodging flying saucers as I went. It was easy to find my quarry because as I ran the lights grew brighter and still brighter until they filled the hanger with a moving rainbow of colors that must mean something important was about to happen.

Thom or Jack would know what they meant but they weren't around.

I stopped before reaching the huge saucer that was emitting the lights because something – some instinct – told me not to get too close. I hung back and watched from behind a different saucer several rows away. I stood behind one of the humongous struts that held it in place.

Even from that distance I felt something. I didn't

know what it was but the feeling grew stronger the brighter those lights became until I knew I should leave.

Something was going on that I didn't understand. Reluctantly, I stepped away from the strut I was behind. The moment I lost the protection of the strut, I was pulled towards the saucer with the flashing lights. An unseen force almost swept me off my feet. Only by grabbing the strut again and holding on for dear life was I able to stay put and upright.

A beam of light appeared from the saucer and pointed towards me. Pinned me in its light. Left me to slip from side to side but then it returned to me. I closed my eyes and prayed and held still tighter to the strut to keep from being pulled towards the saucer.

Then the beam of light that was pulling me along with all the other colored lights that had filled the hanger suddenly winked out of existence. The pull on me ceased. The release of tension was so abrupt I almost fell. In its place there was a thrumming in the floor.

Whatever I'd come to see was happening. As I watched from behind that strut, I knew what it was. The saucer was about to take off. I was nearby. It was a huge craft with power such as I'd never experienced or even imagined before. Was I in danger?

I ran, dodging saucers as I went, glad the tractor beam was no longer pulling me towards it. But before I reached the platform the saucer moved. It lifted as silently as it had done everything else. As silently as the one I'd been in.

When it cleared the parked saucers, it stopped for half a minute and floated mere feet above them. Then in a sudden, silent move it flew towards a hatch that opened as it approached.

Beyond I could see the room where Jack and I had landed with the ocean lapping at the edge of the landing strip but the sight was short-lived because in seconds the saucer dropped into the ocean and the hatch shut.

I was once again alone in the hanger. Stunned. Afraid. Glad I was alive.

I made my way back to the platform, climbed the stairs, and turned back to look over the saucers still parked. They were awesome and I had no wish to walk among them any longer. I was glad the saucer hadn't done to me whatever it had been programmed to do. What that was, I had no idea and doubted that neither Thom or Jack knew.

I left the hanger and went straight to the observation room but I didn't see the saucer that had just taken off. It had only been minutes, but it was gone. The sky was blue and empty.

I stayed there for a long time gazing over the Antarctic Ocean. The day was bright, and the sea was blue and the clouds were white as if nothing out of the ordinary had happened.

I dropped onto one of the couches and realized my stomach was reminding me that it was lunch time so I went to the kitchen and checked the clock there since it was my only way of knowing time. Yes, it was time to eat. I pulled out a frozen dinner, heated it in the microwave, and sat down to a lonely meal. Before I started to eat, Thom entered and soon joined me with a microwaved meal of his own.

He was talkative. "You missed something interesting." He once more used a fork as a baton, something I figured he did on a regular basis. "One of the largest saucers went on patrol a while ago." He used his fork to eat for a bit, then waved it again in the air. "I'd have invited you to watch but I didn't know it was going to happen. We never know. Like I said, they are autonomous and come and go on some unknown predetermined schedule."

"I might have seen it."

"You were in the observation room?"

"Yes." It wasn't a lie because I had been there, just not when the saucer took off.

"Good thing you were there instead of in the hanger when it went airborne. You'd have been in trouble. But it would have been interesting to watch. It's a pretty sight and it's safe as long as you stay on the platform and don't get too close to the saucer that's going aloft."

"Why is that?" What trouble could my curiosity have gotten me into?

"The saucers are evidently programmed to take anything on board that's close and alive, something we learned the hard way. You'd have been swept up by a tractor beam and would even now be cruising somewhere in space."

I choked on my lunch and the resulting commotion made a reply unnecessary which was good because there was no way I'd have been able to say anything without Thom figuring out what had happened. I'd almost been sucked into a flying saucer and who knew how long it would be gone or whether it had rations on board. Probably not.

I could have died if not for the strut that I held as hard as I knew how. I vowed never to go into the hanger alone again. Or at least to not leave the platform that Thom had just informed me was the safe part of the place.

Thom's phone rang. He answered briefly, then clicked it off. "Jack is on his way back. He'll be here momentarily. The saucer is obeying his every command so it appears we now have one more of the largest saucers to add to our inventory of usable craft." He was pleased. "Want to watch him arrive? It's not as spectacular as when a saucer heads out on autonomous patrol but it's interesting enough."

I shouldn't want to go back to that hanger. It was a dangerous place. I'd learned that the hard way. But that was the thing about this fascinating place. Everything that happened in this place was interesting and worth watching.

Besides I did want to see Jack again and I was oddly glad he'd be around for the remainder of my stay at the facility. Because he was the one familiar thing in an unfamiliar place? "Sure. I'd like that."

So once more I stood on that platform and together, we watched Jack's saucer rise from the ocean and skim across the landing strip and then through that hatch. It flew over the parked saucers to the farthest side of the hanger and dropped into an open spot. Soon a door opened and a ramp slid into place and Jack walked down it and across the hanger to join us.

"Good job, Thom," he said, glancing at me beside Thom. "The saucer you worked on is good to go."

They then headed to one of the occupied offices near the hanger. "Book work. You can watch if you're interested but it's kind of boring." Thom's offer was generous but I said I'd see them for dinner and spent the remainder of that day wandering through a labyrinth of corridors getting a feel for the size and scope of the facility.

It was truly awesome, and I could only guess at the beings that had created it and what was in their minds when they first flew their craft through that hatch and into the ocean on the first legs of their journeys. I wish I knew where those journeys ended but I'd never know except in my imagination.

CHAPTER SEVEN

AT BREAKFAST THE next morning I asked Jack where his rooms were located. "In case I need something." I reminded him I didn't have a cell phone.

"Across the hall from you." I finished breakfast in chagrined silence and ignored the laughter in his eyes. It never quite reached his lips, for which I was grateful. "But Thom says the saucer is almost flight worthy so you won't be here much longer."

"I'll be glad to leave." Sort of. My short stay was memorable. I picked at my food and wondered why I was suddenly depressed. "Though this place is amazing, and I'll never forget being here or anything about the facility or the saucers."

That laughter disappeared as if it had never existed. "I suggest you do forget it ever happened and that you forget every single thing you saw here." He leaned across the table and stared at me intently. My insides turned queasy. "You must forget everything about this place. The saucers. Thom. And me. You must. Do it because forgetting is important."

Forget Jack? Never. And the saucers? "You're asking the impossible."

He leaned back and considered me as Thom

entered the dining area. His expression said he'd overheard and he came directly to our table and sat across from me, next to Jack. "He's right, <u>Elena</u>. Secrecy is important. Can you imagine what would happen if the world finds out about this place? About flying saucers?"

"That's the reason I can't forget. Because it's so awesome." I stared at them both and crossed my arms. "But that doesn't mean I'll ever say anything because I won't. I do know how to keep a secret."

Somehow, we ended up eating breakfast. We ate in a not quite companionable silence until I asked, "What about the rest of the people who work here? Jack said they have families. Surely, they can't keep everything secret from people they live with."

Thom replied. "The families do know about this facility, and they know what their family member who works here does but that knowledge is general. Nothing specific. They know that we deal with experimental aircraft, nothing more."

He looked about the room and I could see him thinking about those employees who'd be here if not for being on vacation or on patrol. Or staying away because I was there. "Only after someone is hired do they learn what they are getting into. They also learn that secrecy is important. And they know they can bring their families to my island in the Bahamas. They can live there even if not here. It's quite comfortable." He pointed a spoon at me. "It's nice there and they get to know the other families. It works."

"What about the ones who decide not to work for you once they know the terms?"

"There are no such people."

I found that hard to believe. "You mean everyone who's been offered employment has agreed to everything you just described?"

He shook his head. "They don't know the details until they've decided the lifestyle works for them. Even then they only learn what we do in increments. By the time they know the whole story, they've already been working for the company for well over a year. Only then do they come to this facility instead of working out of the one in Wyoming and only then can their families move to the Bahamas."

Jack took over. "You are the only person not employed by Thom to come here and see what we do. That makes you unique."

Thom added, "And very, very special." He finished his cereal and took his dishes to the kitchen and then returned and straddled a chair to give me a severe look. "Just for transparency's sake and so you'll know what we've been doing while you've been here, by now we know everything about you. Where you were born, where you went to school, how smart you are, everything about your family, who your friends are, what college you were headed to when your car was destroyed in an avalanche, and how trustworthy you are, along with about a thousand other things that are probably irrelevant but that we know anyway." He gave a half smile. "In case you are interested, you passed on all counts. You are one very bright woman, as bright as any of my employees, and you are totally trustworthy as far as we can determine."

Jack finished for him. "That's the reason – and the only reason -- you've been given the run of the place and why we're letting you return to your previous life without restrictions beyond not telling anyone about this place."

"Are you saying you could restrict me in some way? Like a mind wipe?"

"We could try." He shrugged. "Maybe we'd succeed. But we don't feel it's necessary."

Thom rose. "Speaking of getting you back to your previous life, I think I have the damage to the saucer you came in repaired. I want Jack to help me put it through a flight check before I send you away in it. I don't want to sit around and worry while you're gone, I want to know the saucer is safe. Want to come along while we check it out?"

I did.

The flight check was sort of interesting. It would have been interesting if I'd known what they were doing. All I saw was two men asking each other questions and answering those questions in two words or less with their heads stuck either inside of or underneath parts of the flying saucer.

The saucer was sleek and smooth, made of a shiny material capable of repairing itself under the guidance of those lights that seemed to be an integral part of the saucers though they weren't in evidence as Thom and Jack worked.

Thom and Jack were mechanics and would look at a faulty flying saucer engine pretty much the same way my brother Pete would look at the engine in his classic Corvette. They'd all three see pieces of metal that fit together like a jigsaw puzzle.

My brother spent a large part of his life with his head stuck under the hood of whatever classic car he was restoring at the moment, so I recognized Thom's and Jack's posture. My brother was fond of saying I was mechanically challenged and as I listened to the two men discussing things I knew nothing about, I decided he was right.

My mind wandered. Instead of what they were doing, I thought back to those lovely flashing lights. It had been like listening to a beautiful language, only in color instead of sound. If not a language, it was something close. Music, maybe. Visual music, I finally decided.

The lights in the saucer had seemed to be speaking. Or singing. Both the ones that had repaired a hole in its side as I watched and also the lights of the one that flew itself out of the hanger. I was convinced they were similar to a language, though I was pretty sure the two men I was watching would have laughed if I'd said so out loud.

In their defense I did have a huge imagination that tended towards the artistic while they were mechanically minded. As they worked, engrossed in whatever was beneath the control panel, I wished those lights would flash because they were lovely. But they didn't.

My ruminations about lights ended as I realized Thom and Jack were looking at me, waiting for an answer to a question I'd missed because I was remembering lights. "What?" I tried to look like I'd been paying attention. "Could you repeat the question?"

Jack rolled his eyes while Thom patiently repeated his question. "Jack is going to take the saucer for a trial spin. Want to go along?"

"Of course!" The words tumbled out before I had time to think, a bad habit of mine, but this time I was glad because they both seemed pleased at my enthusiasm. "When do we leave?" As if I'd been listening all along. "What do I have to do to get ready?"

"You leave now, and you don't have to do anything. Just give me a minute because I want to get behind the safety shield so I can see what she does up close and personal." A grease monkey at heart, this mechanic also was a genius who wanted to see his baby fly.

As soon as Thom was safely behind what passed for safety glass in this unusual facility – something that would have been nice in the saucer hanger when I was almost kidnapped by a huge flying saucer -- we walked up the ramp and into the saucer. Once in the control room Jack dropped into the captain's chair and rotated a display panel close to his body.

As he passed his hands over the panel in motions that resembled the gestures of an orchestra conductor, those multi-colored lights glowed, the ramp folded in on itself, the door closed, the landing gear retracted and, with a change from multi-colored lights to mostly yellow ones, followed by the blue that seemed to appear when things were ready, the saucer lifted straight up for a few yards, flew horizontally a short distance, and then dropped into the ocean, all without me feeling a thing. Nothing.

I thought about Callie the kitten and how comfortable she'd been in the saucer. No fear of flying because there'd been so sensation of motion. I missed her. I wished she was on Jack's shoulder or mine.

Being in the saucer was weird. I doubted I'd ever get used to it. The sea rushing past was followed by an abrupt ascent from water into air and then high into the sky all in a matter of seconds.

As I watched a blue sea turn to a bright sky, I realized I'd not ride in one ever again after leaving the facility. The thought left me strangely depressed. I had a sudden very strong wish to stay and ride the saucers forever. Perhaps into deep space. Jack said they were capable of deep space flight. Would they ever go that far? I didn't know and never would because I was an outsider.

I thought we'd circle the island and return. Instead, we circled the earth. Not a true circle, we took more of an elliptical course, flying near the earth where it was night and heading way out into space where the sun would have revealed our presence. Prickles went along my spine when the saucer swept into darkness. "Is this safe?"

Jack left the control panel to join me at the window. "Safe as a baby's crib." He pointed to the unblinking stars. "Pretty." I agreed and he came closer, taking my shoulder to turn me in a different direction. "There," he said. "Recognize those stars?"

I'm not an astronomer. I didn't want to appear stupid and was pretty sure that's what was about to happen. Then I saw the Big Dipper. Everyone knows the Big Dipper. "Yep." I found myself relaxing against Jack's chest because his hand was still on my shoulder lightly.

He didn't push me away and we stood that way for a long time, until he spoke, as if coming back from somewhere far away, and said, "Better get back to business and make sure this baby is doing what she should." He returned to the control panel.

The lights flashed. I thought Jack did something

until I noticed his frown and the way he leaned closer to examine the panel. I opened my mouth to ask if something was wrong. Then I shut it just as quickly because if something was wrong the last thing he needed was a curious passenger pestering him with questions. Then I wondered if I should be getting hysterical because we were somewhere in space. No way to call for help. The astronauts on the ISS wouldn't respond.

I waited quietly as Jack passed his hands over the control panel several times, forgetting I existed, and then as suddenly as the lights had come on, they blinked off and whatever had happened was done. "Was it bad?" was all I asked.

He looked up, remembering I was there. "Not too bad. Just a hiccup. It's good now." But I wasn't sure he was telling the truth. In the few days since meeting Jack, I'd come to know him better than almost anyone previous in my life and whatever had happened had been concerning. Enough to delay my return to my life?

Should I tell him I didn't buy his explanation? If I did, would I be brushed aside like a bothersome fly? Yes, I would. This was his saucer and his expertise but I decided to see if I knew him as well as I thought and if he'd reply as I expected. "You're a good liar, Jack. Something was truly wrong, and you fixed it. That's the truth, isn't it?"

He left the control panel and joined me just as he'd done when the fighter jets threatened the saucer. This time, though, he had a frown across his brow and his lips were pressed together. For a moment. Then he shook his head and stuck his tongue out at me. "Think you're pretty bright, don't you? Think you know me?

Think you can trip me up?"

I stuck my tongue out at him. "Yep." And we were laughing, and he was shaking his head and rolling his eyes. But he answered my question. "I was afraid it was bad, I'll admit that. I brought you all the way out here into space to show off a bit and then something happened, and I had you with me and was responsible for you and something went wrong and all I could think was that I'd be to blame if we didn't get back safely and on time." He rubbed the back of his neck in that trademark gesture. "But it wasn't bad after all, though it was due to pure luck and Thom's expertise."

He was telling the truth, it was in his eyes, that he'd been concerned but wasn't now. "Thanks," was all I could think to say. "Thanks for bringing me out here in the first place and thanks in advance for getting me back safely." I thought a moment. "Which you will do. You will get me back safely. Won't you?"

We stared at one another until I broke contact and turned once more to the vastness of space. Then he answered. "I will. I promise."

"But, even if it is dangerous, I love being out here. I wish I could stay forever. I'll miss it."

"I'd miss it too if I couldn't see the stars from space ever again."

"There's no way I can come again? Just to visit?"

"Sorry but the answer is 'no.' You are a one-time phenomenon, the only person ever who doesn't work here who's actually seen and experienced what we do."

With which he returned to the control panel and waved his hands over it and soon we headed back toward earth and the facility. I stayed at the window the entire return trip, wishing I, too, could fly into space on a regular basis and see the stars without the haze of atmosphere in between.

When we landed and Thom and Jack had time to consult with each other and the numerous monitors Thom had been watching, it was decided that I could return to life as I knew it.

"Time to go," Thom said in a hearty voice that showed how concerned he'd been with my visit and how glad he'd be to get rid of me. "Gather your things and you guys can get going tomorrow morning."

I tried to picture the return trip. "Will the saucer put me down in some remote area and I'll have to hitch-hike to civilization?"

They both laughed. "Jack will take you to our facility in the Bahamas. We have a very nice airport there and he'll fly you home in a normal plane and then he'll stick around until you have a replacement car and wardrobe and anything else you need that you lost in the avalanche." He snapped his fingers. "And just like that you'll be back to living your life."

Jack spoke. "It's been interesting having you here. Unusual." Then, as if the words were dragged out of him, "I'll miss you."

He walked me back to my room to gather my things. It felt more like a rejection than a return to normalcy.

CHAPTER EIGHT

THE NEXT MORNING, no one seemed in any hurry to get rid of me. But eventually we headed to the landing strip with my new clothes stuffed into a backpack. Once in the saucer I dropped it on the floor and looked around. I saw Callie. "She wanted to say goodbye," Jack said as the kitten told me she wanted to ride my shoulder.

"I'll miss her. I'll miss everything." I didn't know how to express what I was feeling because my emotions were completely skewed. I said the most inane thing possible. I repeated what Jack had said. "It's been interesting." A complete understatement but I hoped he understood.

Jack's head tipped as he considered Callie and me. "If you were like most people who ended up in a strange situation you'd be so eager to get out of here you'd be pushing buttons to get this thing going. Instead, you're saying you'll miss us and this isn't the first time you've said so. Sounds like you actually like this ugly place."

"I do, though I agree that it's one of the most military-type places I've ever been in. Even the saucer is more homey than the facility." Jack moved towards the control counsel. "Especially when the lights appear. They are lovely."

"We're still trying to figure them out. We think they are monitors of some kind but we suspect they also have a secondary purpose and we don't have a clue about that."

He was a mechanic. I was the artistic type. Colors were part of my life and my future career. "The colors are predictable. There are all different colors at the beginning that turn into just blue when it's done."

"So, you noticed it too."

"I wish they'd put on a light show now."

But the lights never appeared and the trip through the ocean and then through the atmosphere went smoothly with me watching the world through the windows with Callie on my shoulder giving a running commentary on the clouds below while keeping my neck warm and messing with my hair.

As the shadow of night crawled across the world below, I realized why Thom had suggested leaving when we did. Because doing so would mean it would be night when we arrived at his private island so the saucer would be less likely to be seen.

We landed there the same way we landed at the facility, by dropping into the ocean and coming up from the water onto a landing field in a cave. The door opened, the ramp unfolded, and we could leave. Jack made sure we brought my few possessions because I'd never again be inside a flying saucer and I'd need those things in my new life, which was my old life only with amazing experiences added.

The island appeared deserted. "I thought you said families live here."

"Guess they are all somewhere else at the moment." We climbed into a Jeep and headed towards a building that resembled a resort more than a top-secret facility. Totally different from the Antarctic facility, it was actually scenic.

Beyond the main building several picturesque houses straggled along a single street but, again, I didn't see anyone. Not a single person. "It's not a large community," Jack said, almost defensively. "The flying saucer business – the Atlas Project -- doesn't need many people. Besides, it's summer vacation so maybe with school out they all decided to visit relatives."

We left the island the following day. I expected a normal plane. I didn't expect a corporate jet complete with Atlas on the side followed by LLC in elegant letters just like a corporate logo and I definitely didn't expect Jack to be the pilot though, when I thought about it, why shouldn't he know how to fly a jet? He flew flying saucers. A jet was probably child's play.

Once we were airborne, we flew low enough compared to our trip in the saucer that I could make out the ocean below. It was dotted with islands that were visible through occasional breaks in the fluffy, white clouds. "We're in the Bermuda Triangle, aren't we?"

"It is and to answer the question you are about to ask, yes, we are most likely some of the weird things people see in the area. But they've been seeing weird things for hundreds of years and Thom hasn't owned the island that long."

"But the saucers have been flying seemingly forever."

"We don't know if the saucers are behind the Bermuda Triangle mystery or not. What we do know is that the mystery is a good cover story because whenever someone sights one of our saucers everyone just kind of nods and says that's normal for around here."

We landed at a private airport near the closest city to my college and transferred my things to a waiting rental car. We didn't head to my college dorm right away, though. Instead, we headed for a car dealership and when we left, I was the proud owner of a slightly used red Bronco that was way better than the car the avalanche had destroyed. I didn't ask how Jack had managed the insurance because I was pretty sure he hadn't bothered with it.

Then we headed for a shopping mall and when we left the Bronco was loaded with everything a new college student could wish for and more. Then we finally headed for my college and the dorm room I'd been assigned.

Jack helped carry everything. I soon learned that I had two roommates. We'd never met so it was kind of awkward but they managed to give Jack the once-over even though they said nothing to him, just introduced themselves to me and said the usual things about hoping we all had a good summer and wasn't the weather hot and there was a get-together that evening and I was invited. They made sure I understood I could bring Jack while silently letting him know they were available if I wasn't his type.

It all seemed sophomoric and juvenile after riding a flying saucer around the earth and through the ocean and seeing the stars in a black night sky. I looked to Jack for help getting out of a gathering I didn't want to attend, and he came through like a trooper. "I didn't know there'd be a get-together when you arrived. I have reservations for the two of us in town."

"That was thoughtful of you," I said thankfully. "A quiet dinner sounds good after a long trip." The roommates bought it and Jack, and I left as soon as my things were stuffed into drawers and boxes.

Their eyes followed him as we left and when we got into his rental car, I saw them at the dorm window watching. "Thanks, Jack. I really didn't want to attend some idiot group event. And by the way did you know you're a hunk? They drooled over you."

He chuckled. "You should have seen your face when they invited you. I thought you were going to puke. Pretending to have dinner reservations is no big deal. We can find something to eat somewhere, and you can thank me later for saving you from a fate worse than death. As to the hunk thing, I'm guessing your new roommates are so starved for male companionship that anything looks good."

We bought takeout and found a park beside a river where we ate and talked. Then we talked some more. When we finally slowed down enough to pay attention to our surroundings, we realized it was totally dark.

I returned to the dorm to find the girls already asleep. I tiptoed around and found myself at that window watching Jack leave from the same window they'd watched us earlier. As his car pulled away, I felt a sudden, unexpected physical ache that stunned me.

I'd known ever since Thom told me I could leave that I'd miss the facility and the flying saucers and one small calico kitten, but I hadn't given Jack any thought. After all, he was just a cog in what would undoubtedly turn out to be the strangest experience of my life. He was the man in the flying saucer that kept me from freezing to death but I'd deliberately tried not to think of him as a man and a hunk, just as the right person at the right time.

But as that car turned into the main road, I realized he was more than that. He was important in a way I couldn't immediately internalize. I'd miss him badly. As I stared at the empty space where that car had been parked, I wished I didn't feel any special way about him because I'd never see him again. Ever.

Turned out, 'ever' was two weeks because that was how much time elapsed before he stopped by for a visit. I was staring at the wall and trying to focus on graphic art because the whole reason for my taking a summer session was to get credentials for my future career.

Every time I walked into a classroom filled with the colors and shapes that go with an art class, I remembered the flashing lights of the saucers. Surely there was a reason for them. I just didn't know what it was because I wasn't around long enough to figure it out.

I sighed. Staring at the wall failed to help me understand art any better and did nothing at all to help me with my current graphic design project. Carla, my blonde roommate, was sitting in the window seat and examining the outside world when she sat up straight. "He's here, Elena."

I looked up. "Who's here?"

"Your boyfriend."

"I don't have a boyfriend."

She laughed. "Yes, you do. The whole boyfriend, girlfriend thing was clear as day when he brought you here. Your gain, my loss." She sighed and looked outside again. "And here he is." Her eyebrows rose. "A surprise visit?" She glanced at Sherie, the brunette roommate. "Maybe we should leave to give them privacy."

"Not necessary," I said hastily as I ran to the window to see for myself because she must be mistaken. But she was right, Jack was headed towards the door. "He's not my boyfriend, we don't need privacy, and I have no idea why he's here."

Turned out he just happened to be in the area and decided to see how I was doing. I learned that fact after he drove us to once again get some takeout and return to that same park we'd been to before because, as he said, it was as nice as any place.

"You just happened to be in the area?" I gave him my most suspicious look. "Like on Earth instead of Mars? Is that what you call being in the area?"

He laughed so hard he choked on his fried chicken. "Believe it or not, I do occasionally find myself in various places on Earth. We do need supplies and not many places make deliveries to the Antarctic. Anyway, as long as I was nearby, I decided to check up on a friend." After getting past the choking, he waved his chicken leg much as Thom had waved his silverware to make a point. "We are friends, aren't we, and visiting is okay, isn't it?" When I assured him we were and that a visit was appreciated, he continued. "How's the summer going? Well, I hope."

"It sucks." I decided to be honest. "I see stars and the curve of the earth instead of whatever I'm supposed to be studying." I watched the nearby river make its way to the ocean. "The thing is, I'm not sure I'll ever get over what happened. Some things are too awesome to forget."

I turned from the river to Jack. "And that's really why you're here, isn't it? To check on me. To make sure I haven't told anyone about the facility or the flying saucers because you know I can't forget them. But mostly you're here because what you do is so important that you don't dare trust anyone so someone will be checking on me forever."

He put down his chicken and came close and wrapped an arm around me. The gesture was so unexpected that I had no time to put up mental or emotional armor against him. How did he know I wanted to cry at the thought of never again flying higher than jets can go?

I leaned into him as I'd done on the saucer and we stayed that way for a long time, Jack saying nothing because there was nothing to say and me wishing there were words for what I was experiencing. But at least he understood. And his body felt wonderful against mine.

He finally spoke. "I felt the same way the first time I went home after flying above the earth. I couldn't tell anyone about it, and it was hard to say nothing. I can't say how long it will take for you to feel normal again. All I can say is that I hope it will happen."

We stayed beside that river until long after dark but after my little outburst our conversation was subdued because underneath everything we said was the undeniable truth that I'd experienced something so secret I'd never be able to talk about it while being unable to forget it.

As he walked me to my door in the middle of the night, he said, "I'll be back. Not to make sure you're not spilling any secrets because we trust you. Just to visit." Before he turned to leave, he added, "If it's okay with you."

I told him I'd look forward to any visits and when I entered my dorm room I moved as quietly as possible so as not to wake my roommates though I didn't sleep that night. Instead, I stared out the window at the starry sky and thought about flying saucers and the man who flew them. Especially the man who flew them.

He stopped by twice more during the brief summer school session. Each time was pretty much a repeat of that first visit except that each time he stayed longer than the time before because we found more to talk about. The last time he visited we watched the sun rise over that river and it was almost as beautiful as when it rose over the edge of the earth and was seen from space.

Still, I couldn't stop feeling depressed because I'd go through life knowing about flying saucers and little kittens and colors that meant something special though I'd never see any of them again. But I never admitted those thoughts to Jack, not even the time we stayed up all night. Instead, I told him that normalcy was returning and I'd be fine eventually. He didn't believe me, of course, because by then he knew me as well as I knew him. But there was nothing either of us could do about it.

CHAPTER NINE

BEING HOME BETWEEN the end of the summer session and the beginning of the fall one was good because it was normal and normalcy is calming. But though the world around me was normal, I wasn't, not even close, and everyone noticed.

"Do you want to talk?" my mother asked in her best mother-daughter voice because a new-to-me red SUV had required an explanation.

"Maybe you should see a counselor." From my practical father.

"You're pretty whacked out," my brother Pete announced. The fact that he noticed even though his head was stuck under the hood of the Corvette he was restoring said a lot. He was in our garage because his apartment had no place to work on cars. "Better get your head on straight or who knows what Mom and Dad might do and, no, you can't come live with me to get away from them."

At which moment a strange car turned into the driveway. Pete brought his head out long enough to check out the newcomer in case it was someone he knew. He was about to stick it back beneath the hood because the car was strange when he noticed the look on my face. Then he kind of stepped in front of me to protect me from whomever was climbing out of that car because surely it was someone dangerous based on the stunned look on my face.

"It's a friend," I said quietly so Jack wouldn't hear as he approached Pete and me beside the Corvette. Then Jack noticed the Corvette and walked past me and straight to Pete. "Sweet," he said. "I always wanted one."

He asked what Pete was doing beneath that hood and just like that they were instant buddies. It was a good thing I didn't need protecting because Pete would have thrown me away in an instant in favor of someone who could talk cars and soon afterwards my dad joined them, having noticed the strange car in the driveway and come to check it out.

They three were mechanics, just like Thom and Jack at the facility only with cars instead of flying saucers. But after a couple minutes Jack – reluctantly, I thought – turned away from the Corvette to focus on me. "Can we talk?"

"Sure." Though I was mystified as to what there was to talk about because I was pretty sure he'd not mention flying saucers because that would make it harder for me to forget what had happened.

"Somewhere private," he added as Pete and my dad surfaced and listened in on the conversation.

My dad looked from Jack to me. "Who is this person?"

"This is Jack. The guy who rescued me when the avalanche buried my car."

Before leaving the facility Thom, Jack and I had concocted a story about my missing days that was as true-to-life as possible. In the story my car was buried by an avalanche just as a life-ending blizzard approached but I was saved by a man named Jack who happened along and brought me to safety at the top-secret facility where he worked in order to save my life and I stayed there until the blizzard ended.

The story was mostly true but without flying saucers. Instead, in the story Jack drove a truck and the facility was nearby but since it did top-secret stuff, I couldn't tell anyone anything about it.

Now, before my dad could properly react to Jack showing up, my mom burst out of the house, having overheard, and threw her arms around him. "Thank you, thank you, thank you for saving Elena's life."

When Jack managed to disentangle himself, he repeated his question. "Can we talk? Privately?" When I didn't respond, he added, "Thom wants me to give you a message. It's personal."

"Thom?" My father wanted to know who Thom was. Jack explained that he managed the top-secret facility. "Does this Thom have the government's permission to speak? I don't want Elena to get in trouble because someone said something they shouldn't."

Jack explained that Thom owned the company and that it was a small, private company that contracted with the government so the government had little say over how Thom managed it. So Jack and I took a walk to a small cove of oaks bordering the field beside our house that was frequented by biology classes during the day and teenagers at night.

When the trees closed around us and we found a downed tree to substitute for a bench, I waited for Jack to talk. I couldn't imagine what Thom wanted him to tell me.

Jack didn't bother with small talk. "Thom wants to hire you. Do you want to work with us?"

The offer was so unexpected I was unable to speak. My mouth dropped as I tried to wrap my mind around the idea. "Me? Work for you?"

"For Thom, actually, since he owns the business."

"At the facility?"

"That's where we work. It's our base."

"Why me? You and Thom are mechanics. I don't know one engine part from another."

"Thom checked you out thoroughly and says you're extremely intelligent and learn quickly and are dependable and you liked the saucers and were interested in what we are doing." He lifted his hands as if that explained everything. "He thinks you're perfect."

"I'm still in school. No degree."

"Thom can hire anyone he wants, degree or not."

Sunlight shining through the oak leaves dappled his face, making it difficult to read his thoughts. "Is this a way of keeping tabs on me to make sure I won't reveal any secrets? Because if it is, I promise I can keep quiet. You don't have to bribe me."

"I agree that if you work for him then he won't have to worry about disclosure. But it's more important that while you were there you liked what you saw. You said you'd miss it and we believed you. As far as Thom is concerned, interest outweighs everything else. You want to do what we do and you're bright and that's the main qualification and you've been to the facility so that's what decided Thom to offer you a job."

"I don't know anything about flying saucers."

"None of us did when we were hired so as to that

you'd be no different. You'll be taught what you need to know, and you can get any college degree you want through online courses, like the rest of us have done. Thom will foot the bill because he wants his employees to be knowledgeable in as many fields as possible."

"What if I'm a lousy employee? I'm not a mechanic and I'll never understand how machinery works and all I saw you two do while I was there was fix things."

"You don't have to know what makes a car run in order to drive it from one place to another." He rubbed the back of his neck. "As Thom said that first day, we still don't know everything about the saucers but we fly them anyway and we learn more all the time."

"I'm stunned."

"Of course, you are. It hits all of us that way when we find out what we were actually hired to do. It's a lot to think about and I don't expect an answer now. I'll be back in the area in a week or so. I'll stop by then and maybe you'll have an answer."

"What if I don't want to work for Thom? Will something bad happen to keep me quiet?"

"I promise there is nothing coercive about this offer. You learned about some stuff while you were there, and it didn't freak you out. That made Thom look at you as a possible employee."

We sat on that log for a while longer, but the gist of the visit was done. I was being offered a job that would take me into space. If I accepted, I'd see the stars against the black of space instead of through the prism of the atmosphere. I'd ride a flying saucer to places people had never been. It would be awesome.

On the flip side, I'd not be able to tell anyone

about my job and I'd spend most of my off days in a remote, windowless facility buried in an island in the Antarctic Ocean.

"I'll do it. I accept."

"Not so fast. Give yourself a week. More if needed. It's important that if you decide to take the job you do so after having thought it through, so you know what's involved. We don't want you to have regrets later."

"What can I tell my family while I'm waiting for your return?"

"That you've been offered a top-secret job so you can't divulge any information about the job itself or anything connected to it."

"Understood."

We returned to the house. As we passed from the oaks into the field and then to the place where I'd lived my entire life, the sun hit Jack's face full on and I could read his expression easily. Every word he'd said was the truth.

Thom wanted me to become a part of what Jack had called the Atlas Project. I liked the name. Thom believed I would fit in, and he was a genius who knew his business and he thought I had the proper skills. That was all that mattered.

Jack left as soon as we returned, leaving me to face my family. "So, what was that all about if you care to let us know?" So, I told them.

At first, they didn't know how to react. When they'd recovered their equilibrium, they pretty much repeated the things I'd already told Jack. That I was too young, didn't have a degree, didn't know a thing about the world and so on until there was nothing left to say and we all kind of limped into the house where we drank lemonade and stared at one another and tried to come to grips with the change that was about to happen to the family.

Because we all knew I'd take the job. It was in my face, my entire demeanor, and Pete's words finally put the whole thing into focus. "We don't know anything about this really odd business, and we never will know but that's irrelevant because it's what you're going to do." He struggled with the idea. "So, all we can do is congratulate you and hope you're making the right decision."

Normally we saw Pete once or twice a week. That week he came over every day. He said it was to work on the Corvette. Actually, it was to find out if anything had changed since the previous day's visit. As he worked on the Corvette and I watched, he worked slower and slower until he gave up pretending to do anything and shut the hood and confronted me. "I gather that your friend Jack is a pretty good mechanic." I agreed. "Will that ability be needed in your new job? Because if it will you won't work there very long."

"Jack uses his mechanical skills in his job but Thom said it won't be necessary for me. There must be other jobs."

"Just checking. I don't want my baby sister to be fired soon after she's hired." Curiosity was clear in his face. He wanted to know about my future job but knew he couldn't ask.

"I don't have a clue what I'll be doing so wipe that look off your face. All I can do is believe that Thom knows what he's doing in offering me a job."

"Your friend Jack looks healthy and financially

comfortable.”

"He is."

"So, you will be too, I presume."

"Thom is filthy rich and spends all his time and money on the business and his employees."

"He sounds like a fanatic."

"He is."

My parents joined us, and we did what we'd done ever since Jack's visit. We waited for him to return.

CHAPTER TEN

IT WAS A full week before Jack returned. His arrival was a repeat of his first visit. Different rental car, same turn into the driveway followed by a quick survey of the place and a walk to where Pete was working on the Corvette. He didn't turn to me until they ran out of things to discuss about restoring old cars.

Then he simply asked, "Can we talk?" Followed by, "Is the oak grove available?"

We crossed the field with Pete watching with arms crossed and curiosity in his demeanor. I was pretty sure my parents were also watching from the kitchen window. But we disappeared from everyone's view the instant we stepped into the grove. We walked until we found that same downed tree and settled on it side by side. Not too close, not too far apart.

We both sensed that everything had to be carefully orchestrated because this was going to be an important discussion. We gave ourselves time to take in the sights, to listen to the rustling of the leaves and the squirrels as they ran along the branches above us, and to think what to say. Because we both wanted to get this right.

Jack began. "It's been a week. Was that enough?

Do you need more time?"

"No more time. I accept Thom's offer."

He nodded without looking at me. "Don't be too quick to accept. There's more. Something I didn't mention before. I've been thinking about it ever since I told you about Thom's offer. I should have spoken earlier and I'm sorry I didn't."

"More?"

"Something else you should know. You might change your mind."

"More?" My lack of mechanical skills was the most likely problem. "I thought you said it didn't matter that I'm not mechanical."

"It's not that."

"Then what?"

"Me. The problem is me."

"You?"

"Thom wants you to work for him. I'm not sure you'll want to do that once I tell you what I should have told you earlier."

That first day when he walked through that holographic doorway in the saucer and saw me standing in the hall, he'd been angry. I was an intruder and shouldn't have been there. But that anger had faded when he realized how and why I'd crawled through the hole in the saucer's side. At least I'd thought it had. Now I wasn't so sure.

"I thought we were friends. You said we were." I tried to wrap my mind around what he was telling me. "If you don't like me, why didn't you say so? Why let me think were okay with each other?"

"We are okay. We are friends. It's not that."

"Then what?"

"I do like you."

"So, what's the problem?"

"I like you very much and that's the problem. I like you very, very much. Maybe too much. You might not be comfortable with that." He rubbed the back of his neck and the gesture sent goosebumps along my spine. "The thing is, if you and I are in close proximity I'll be wanting to hit on you every chance I get and I can't imagine not doing so unless you physically chase me away and I don't know where I'll go if you do that because there's no way to leave the facility and I don't know where you'd go to get away from me if you need space. But I don't want you to hate me, either. So you can see that it's a problem."

"You like me? A lot?"

He dropped his hands between his knees and bent over and avoided me by staring at them. "I want you in my life so badly I can taste it."

"You never said anything."

"I thought I'd never see you again so it didn't matter how I felt. I'd get over you in time. But having you near me on a daily basis, perhaps even working with me, that'll be totally different." He straightened and turned towards me. "I can't imagine what it'll be like for either of us in such circumstances."

The space between us snapped with energy. "I don't know either." Didn't have a clue.

"Well now you know how things are and it can make a difference. So think it over. But, like last time, don't make a decision now. Take this new information into consideration and spend more time deciding whether you want to work for Thom." He rose and waited for me to join him, carefully not coming any closer. "I know this is unexpected."

"It is." It was mind-blowingly unexpected.

"Take time to think. All the time you need. I'll stop by in --- when do want me to return?"

I stepped close. Looked at him and made sure he was looking back. Felt the pull between us and wondered why I'd not felt it before. Yes, I decided as I stared into those blue eyes, I had felt it, I'd just not recognized it for what it was. The man-woman thing. "Come back soon."

"I'll be back in a week." He rubbed the back of his neck again. "But you don't have to know by then. You can take as long as you need to decide."

"One week." Inside of me I already knew what my decision would be and that fact stunned me though I felt a growing anger at him for waiting until now to tell me how he felt. But I was amazed at some level that it didn't take time for me to think through what this meant. I already knew.

I must have sensed something while we were at the facility without that knowledge rising to a conscious level. What Jack said was true about the isolated nature of the facility magnifying everything, including emotions, but of course we'd suppressed them for the very same reason they were magnified now. We'd been thrown together in an isolated place.

Only now had his words brought all that to my consciousness but as soon as he spoke, I knew what I wanted. I wanted flying saucers. And I wanted Jack. But I also knew it would do no good to tell him my decision now because he'd still insist on me taking time to think things through. I was kind of shocked that I knew him well enough to know that about him. "One week will be more than enough."

"One week, then. I'll see you in a week."

We walked back through that field as sedately apart as when we'd come and when we reached the house he didn't stay to visit, not even briefly.

"What was that all about?" Pete asked after Jack was gone. "He didn't even say goodbye." He looked me over. "Did you refuse the job?"

"There was more to the job than what he said earlier. He's giving me a week to think it over with this new information added to what I already knew."

"So we go through this agony for another week? All of us, the whole family? We all have to tip-toe around you while you think?"

"Is that what you did?"

"Of course." He gave me a big brother look. "And we'll do it for one more week. But by then you'd better have decided what you're going to do because one more week is all the tip toeing we can handle."

The family did spend the next week tip toeing around me and I spent that same week deciding what to say and how to act when Jack returned. I already knew what I wanted but wasn't sure how to tell him. But when he turned into the driveway precisely one week to the day later in still a different rental car, I was prepared.

Once more we crossed the field to that oak grove and disappeared into the shade where the family couldn't watch even though I knew they were going crazy not knowing what was going on. For a third time we dropped onto that fallen tree only this time I waited until Jack was seated before sitting myself. Then I sat so close that if we'd been any closer, we'd have been touching. But we remained two separate beings staring straight ahead and pretending that doing so was normal.

Jack cleared his throat. "Well? Do you need more time?"

"Nope. No more time needed."

"What's your decision?"

"Same as before. I accept Thom's offer."

He was silent for a long time. "Are you sure?" Said carefully with no inflection at all.

"Totally sure." I let the silence go on for a while and wondered how long I should wait before saying what I'd decided to say. Eventually the birds screaming and the leaves rustling, and the crickets chirping were so insanely loud that I couldn't stand them any longer. "But there's one thing that I do need to know."

"What's that?"

I turned to him. Pulled his face away from those darn birds and towards me. "I want to know what this will feel like." And I pulled him all the way to me and kissed him.

It felt every bit as good as I'd anticipated. When I'd been deciding how to handle this meeting I'd planned on telling him how great it was when the kiss ended but I didn't get the chance because less than a second after that kiss ended he wrapped his arms around me and pulled me close and the kissing thing continued only with him being the instigator which was even better because it gave me a feel for the real Jack. I liked what I felt.

Eventually, though, we broke apart and he said, "So now you know what life will be like if you accept Thom's offer."

"I do know, and I approve."

He put a finger on my nose lightly and smiled but his eyes were serious as I managed not to sneeze. "I don't know how serious this thing between you and me is or what will happen in the future but you should know that whatever happens between us will be magnified a thousand times by our unusually close proximity. So be sure you know what you're getting into."

"I'm willing to take a chance if you are."

"I'm definitely willing."

"So, all I need to know is when I report for work."

A smile so broad it almost broke his face accompanied his reply. "I'll find out from Thom. I'm guessing he'll want you there as soon as you can wrap things up here and prepare for the next part of your life." He thought over what he'd said. "The job you're about to take will be almost your entire life. I wonder if, when you find out how things work at the Atlas Project, the tiny bit of time left over will include me."

"It will. I promise."

Walking back across that field and knowing my family was watching even though we couldn't see them we kept carefully separate. This time Jack stayed late because he knew they'd feel better about my decision if someone who was already doing what I'd shortly be doing was there to answer any questions they might have. Though of course there weren't many questions they could ask about a top-secret job.

I thought we hid the man-woman thing pretty well. Turned out I was wrong. I learned that when Jack and my dad were in the kitchen, and I started there to get another can of pop. I stopped when I overheard them talking.

My dad asked, "How hard did you have to push this Thom person to get him to offer Elena a job? Because I'm pretty sure you did. Because you wanted the two of you together."

I held my breath waiting for Jack's reply. I wondered if he blushed easily because if he did, he was probably doing it then. "Thom really did plan on offering her a job no matter what I said."

"But you pushed for it."

"Yes."

"Hard?"

"Yes." Just the one word but it said a lot.

"Just asking, that's all, and you'd better be careful with my little girl." I wanted to hit my dad over the head for that last remark but I refrained because if I did they'd know I was eves-dropping. I wanted to shout that I was capable of taking care of myself, thank you very much, because I was an adult but that was something he'd not yet learned and probably never would and I loved him for it.

It was after midnight when Jack left. I walked him to his car and touched his hand lightly before he shut the door much as he'd touched my nose earlier. It was all I dared do with everyone watching.

Our eyes met but it was too dark to know what he was thinking. He started the engine and pulled away and I watched him go, knowing that soon I'd see him again along with more flying saucers than I could count meticulously lined up in an underground hanger in a secret base on a nondescript island in the Antarctic Ocean that was about to become my home.

CHAPTER ELEVEN

IT TOOK LONGER than expected to wrap up my life. I told friends and family what little I could about my new job, and they promptly told me I was insane. I extricated myself from the college I was committed to, including moving out of a dorm room with two roommates who gave each other knowing looks after I admitted that, yes, I'd be working with the guy they'd called my boyfriend whom I'd insisted wasn't. Then there was a life's collection of possessions to sort through because I only took what would fit in a room like the one I'd been in before. While spacious, it wasn't gigantic, and I guessed it was typical.

The sorting was followed by goodbyes. I'd been assured I could visit home often but it felt like I was leaving forever. As I gazed at the sky through my bedroom window that last night I decided I was feeling the all-encompassing concept of space. Someday I'd be in that sky and would thus be isolated not just from people I knew but from everyone. It was an unsettling feeling even though I badly wanted to be there.

"We all felt that way at first," Jack said as he helped move my stuff from the back of still another rental car to the corporate jet that would take us to the island in the Bahamas. I'd admitted to my feelings in the night and was relieved that he understood.

My family had come along to help carry stuff in the family SUV and say one last goodbye. They were genuinely impressed with the top-of-the-line jet and my brother Pete was positively envious of the fact that Jack was the pilot.

Then we were in the air and Jack gave me the gift of silence as I stared out the window and wondered what I was getting myself into and whether I was smart or stupid to have taken such a truly bizarre job. But as time and miles added up the feeling abated and I watched passing clouds with the awe that always came over me upon seeing them up close and personal.

When we landed at the island in the Bahamas, I saw an island somewhat different from the first time we were there. There were people everywhere. Not hoards of people but enough that I knew my first guess why that many had decided to take vacations earlier was accurate. They disappeared because I was there.

We didn't spend much time there, though, just enough to grab a meal while Jack said 'hi' to people he knew, and they gave me a curious once-over. We transferred my belongings to the saucer in the hanger hidden in a cave on the island. After the ramp retracted and the door closed Jack passed his hands over that control panel in the center of the saucer and in seconds we were in the water and soon after we were above everything and watching the world from unimaginable heights and it all happened without any sensation of motion while being as comfortable as if I was in my parents' living room.

We arrived at the facility on that Antarctic Ocean

Island in what seemed like minutes and couldn't have been much more than that. The speed of our travel made me realize how truly damaged that original saucer must have been that it had taken us the better part of a day to traverse the same distance. We plunged into the ocean in what was now a familiar routine and resurfaced onto that underground landing strip.

Thom was waiting for us with a middle-aged woman with hair starting to gray at her temples and a no-nonsense air about her. They approached and Thom introduced her. "Meet Mazie,"

No preliminary talk. I'd already figured he wasn't the conversational type. "She'll be your tutor. She'll teach you everything you need to know." He thought over what he'd just said and added, "Enough to get you started. In this place learning never ends."

Jack said we should take my things to my room. "Same room as before. Across the hall from me."

"And just down the hall and around the corner from me." Mazie looked me up and down and I wondered what she thought about a too-young upstart recruit but she only said, "I don't know why they don't combine rooms into suites so we'd have more space. There are certainly enough of them, and we are a small and special group of trained astronauts. We deserve a few perks."

She turned to go. "I'll see you in the kitchen after you unpack and we'll work out a schedule for your lessons. If settling in takes a long time, tomorrow will be fine. No hurry in this place. Knowledge first, skill second. Speed will come."

"Knowledge and skill at what?" I asked Jack as we piled my things in the middle of my room, and I looked about to figure where to put everything. "No one has told me exactly what I'll be doing."

"Flying saucers, of course."

"I expected to be assigned to support services. Cooking, cleaning, or something similar."

"No one does those things. We prepare our own meals if we don't want frozen dinners. Which means we mostly do our own cooking. Same goes for cleaning and just about everything else. There are a few robots to do routine stuff. No support staff needed. No unnecessary people to know what we do."

"Everyone here is a saucer pilot?"

"Yep."

"Are there many of you?"

"Not many. You'll meet all of them in time."

The suspicion grew that there'd been people there during my first visit. The place was so huge a convention could have taken place there without me knowing about it and they'd not have had to make even the slightest effort to hide. "I never saw anyone except you and Thom when I was here before."

"We are a busy place. Lots of patrols." Something about his expression said my guess was right and that reminded me of how the island in the Bahamas had also seemed deserted during my previous visit but was full of people upon my return.

"Was everyone told to disappear while I was there? And on the island?"

He stopped unpacking a box of my favorite books and looked directly at me. I liked that about him. That he connected on a personal level and let me read his mind. That he was open. "No sense taking a chance on you recognizing someone at a later date. No telling what would come of it if that happened."

I stopped what I was doing. "The secrecy thing is that important?"

"Yep." The one word said it all. We went back to unpacking but that single word had sucked the fizz from the air.

After putting away my things we adjourned to the kitchen. As I walked in I decided it must be the meeting place for the facility. It was the room for social activity. When we walked through the door, I saw that it wasn't filled to capacity but where before it had been empty now there were only a couple of empty tables and the buzz of conversation could be heard long before we got there.

When we entered, the talk stopped. Heads turned towards us. People getting their dinner stopped whatever they were doing. The inspection was so intense I wished I could drop through the floor. Then Mazie stood up and strode over to us. Grabbed me by the arm and waved to everyone. "This is Elena. She's the new pilot." She amended her statement. "She will be the new pilot when I'm done with her."

That statement was met with cheers and the tension broke, and everyone wanted to know more about me. Where I was from. Whether I was certifiably insane because I wanted to pilot a flying saucer, though they made sure I understood that would make me like everyone else in the room. "We're ghosts," someone in the back said. "You'll be a ghost too."

Someone else said, "Boo!" and they all laughed and this time I did too. But I still felt awkward, and Jack sensed it and steered me to the kitchen where we found a couple of frozen dinners that we heated up and brought to the nearest table that wasn't full.

Mazie joined us. "Forget what I said earlier about making a schedule. Get acquainted today. Ask questions. Get a good night's sleep tonight and tomorrow we'll get that schedule worked out and go from there."

I was glad Jack was there. It soon became clear that I was the youngest person there by several years and probably the youngest recruit Thom had ever hired and that alone made everyone there intensely curious about me. They'd heard how I'd got there in a disabled saucer but they wanted to hear it from me and they wanted the details.

By the time Jack kind of pulled me away from everyone I was feeling better about my decision because these people obviously felt the same way I did about life, space, and flying saucers. But I was also tired, the kind of tiredness that's more emotional than physical and Jack knew that. Of course, he did. He'd been through the same thing and was that kind of guy.

I amended that thought. He was that kind of guy about me and my feelings but I didn't know if he was as astute with other people. I gladly followed him back to our rooms that were across the hall from each other. I was glad he was close. No particular reason, I'm not a wimp, but it just felt good to have someone I knew nearby.

Then I remembered there was still the evening to get through. Hours stretched ahead. Without windows it was easy to forget. "Must I sit in my room all evening?"

"Only if you want to."

"What else is there to do?"

"Want to go for a ride in a saucer? Not to get

anywhere. Just for fun."

"Can we?"

"I think so. It's not too late. I'll ask Thom."

Before we went to find Thom, Jack scooped Callie from where she'd been sleeping on his bed. "She likes to go for rides."

"It doesn't feel like a ride. Being in a saucer feels like we're standing still."

"I suspect that's why she likes it. She can watch the world -- or the moon and stars -- beyond the windows without fear."

We found Thom where I soon learned he was almost always located. In the office beside the landing strip fiddling with a computer while watching a saucer on the screen. "What's up?" he asked while staying focused on the saucer. Multicolored lights flashed around the saucer on the screen, faster and faster until he tapped a key on the computer and the saucer went dark. "We're getting close. It won't be long before we figure out what those lights do other than just look pretty."

"What say I take Elena for a ride? Show her what saucers can do."

Thom turned the computer back on and considered the saucer on the screen. "Good idea." He turned to us. "Take this one that I've been working on. See what she'll do."

"Acrobatics?"

"Absolutely. Push her hard. And do some submerged stuff. Pretend you're a sea creature."

"Can do," Jack said, and we left the office and found the saucer that had put on the light show under Thom's guidance. The saucer door opened, and a ramp unfolded. I looked towards the office and saw Thom fiddling with that computer.

"Can he make saucers do anything he wants?"

"Opening doors and boarding is easy. The rest can be iffy but someday he'll make these saucers dance." The ramp retracted and the door closed. Jack headed for the control panel as Callie left his shoulder and headed for mine. "Let's go."

CHAPTER TWELVE

THE EXIT FROM the facility was normal for a flying saucer which meant it was abnormal for any other flying craft but I knew what would happen because I'd experienced it before. First down into the ocean and then up into the sky. I didn't panic and the kitten on my shoulder enjoyed the scenery. After that, though, things changed.

"This will be fun," Jack said with the kind of lilt that said he'd enjoy what was about to happen. "You'll like it. Or maybe you won't like it but it'll still be interesting. And don't worry, I know what I'm doing. We won't fall out of the sky."

His words should have warned me but no words could have prepared me for what happened next. Not that I knew the difference. Not at first.

"Why did the sky rotate?" Beyond the windows the setting sun was no longer on our left side. Instead, it had flipped as I watched and now was on the right and the earth was above us instead of below where it belonged. "How'd that happen?"

"We turned upside down."

"I'm still standing straight. I'm not upside down."

"Remember me telling you saucers create their own environment? We are in what passes for a small, unique universe that extends millimeters beyond the hull. In that universe we don't obey the rules for the universe beyond the hull. So, we can change direction, height, anything we wish without changing how we are situated inside the saucer, which is our little universe. It's the outside that seems to change, though in reality the outside is where it was all along, and our small universe is moving through it."

"That's insane."

"But it's what happened. Watch." And he did it again. He flipped the saucer. But none of us in the saucer felt movement. Instead, it appeared as if the world rotated back to where it should be. "Now watch some more." That outer world started whirling around and around until I got dizzy just from watching though not from any sensation of movement because there wasn't any inside the saucer. Jack called from the control panel. "Like it?"

"Should you be doing this? Is it dangerous?"

"Thom asked me to do this. Remember?"

"I remember he asked you to test its limits. But that's all he asked. Limits, not beyond limits. So I ask again, are you pushing too hard?"

"Not even close."

We continued the acrobatics for a few minutes. Then he righted the saucer so it once more was aligned with the earth and said, "Now to do the other thing Thom asked."

More acrobatics? Jack grinned widely for a second or so then pulled his face straight and I could tell from his expression that he hoped I hadn't noticed the grin but he hadn't been able to help it. He was enjoying our flight too much to keep a sober face. "Are you ready?"

"I forgot Thom's instructions. What else are we supposed to do?"

"Go into the ocean and play with the fish." With which he waved his hands over the control panel and the scenery beyond the windows suddenly changed as we dropped thousands of feet in seconds but inside it was like watching a movie on a screen except the screen was reality and we were in it.

The plunge into the ocean was so abrupt and smooth I wouldn't have noticed except for the change from blue sky to bluer water. Jack called out from the control panel. "Want to go treasure hunting?"

"How? Where? What kind of treasure?"

"The kind that supports this endeavor. The ocean floor is littered with sunken treasure and since we're here we might as well bring some back."

"How do we get it on board?"

"We don't." Then he used the same phrase he used before the acrobatics. "Watch. It'll be fun."

The ocean was dark and as we went deeper it got darker and then darker still until Jack snapped his fingers at that control panel and lights all around the outside of the saucer suddenly lit up the darkness. Strange fish darted out of the light while others were drawn to it. I pressed closer to the windows to see better because I'd never seen anything so strange. And still the saucer dropped until it hung inches above the ocean floor. I didn't ask how deep we were. I didn't want to know.

Jack joined Callie and me at the window and pointed. "See that?" All I saw was sea creatures and strange shapes lurking on the edge of the lighted area. "Treasure."

"How do you know?"

"We mapped this area some time ago but haven't mined all the treasure yet. We'll get some now."

"How will you do that and how do you know where to look?" Because everything was black and brown and covered with sediment.

"Watch." He mentally measured a space about twenty feet beyond the saucer, then returned to the control panel and gestured. A beam brighter than the lights around the saucer sliced through the sea towards the area he'd indicated.

I recognized the light from science fiction movies. It was a tractor beam. The dark, unrecognizable objects on the edge of the lighted area were caught by the beam and began to move slowly but surely towards the saucer. When they were close, the movement stopped. Then the saucer slowly, slowly rose through the water with the tractor beam securely holding what he'd said was treasure. As we rose ocean water cleaned the things being held, washing away hundreds of years of sediment and exposing furniture from long ago.

"Chests," I said unnecessarily. "Treasure chests?"

"We'll find out when we get back," Jack answered. "Not always. Sometimes we just get sludge that used to be clothes and what's left disintegrates the instant we open the chests." He examined the chests as best he could considering they were outside the saucer and he was inside. "But sometimes we get lucky."

When we returned to the landing strip Thom was waiting as the saucer emerged from the ocean with the tractor beam pulling the chests along. He strolled towards them as the saucer door opened and the ramp unfolded, and Jack and I joined him.

I didn't touch the disgusting things. Jack and Thom had no such qualms and grabbed crowbars and ripped the chests apart. Not that there was much to rip because they disintegrated as soon as the bars touched them. The tractor beam and all that sludge must have been all that was keeping them intact.

It was hard to know what was inside. Mostly black mud. But Thom got a hose and proceeded to clean the contents and then we saw it. "Treasure." I was in awe. "Is that gold?"

"We struck pay dirt," Jack said as he bent over to more closely examine the gold bars shining in the landing strip lights.

"We were in the Antarctic Ocean."

"No, we weren't," Jack said. "Not much treasure in the Antarctic so we took a little trip."

"Halfway around the world?"

"While we were doing somersaults we were also moving right along."

I'd read about treasure hunting. "Isn't it illegal to keep this?"

"They weren't found in any country's territorial waters and there's no way to know what country's ship they were on." He looked at me. "Did you see a name?"

"I couldn't see a ship let alone a name. Just dark blobs."

"Because the ship had already disintegrated. No way to know where it came from."

"So, we're good?"

"We're good."

Jack pulled me away from Thom and the gold bars.

"He'll handle it from here. Now what do you prefer? To stay up and read or get a good night's sleep before you learn how to fly a saucer?"

I opted for sleep and woke up the next morning fresh and ready for lessons. As I showered and dressed it occurred to me that if I'd not taken Thom up on his offer of a job, I'd be doing the same thing at college. But the classes would be quite different.

I went in search of breakfast and Mazie. I found her in the kitchen sipping coffee and waiting. "The first thing you learn is to work the colors."

"Do you mean the flashing lights on the walls of the saucers?"

"Yes, but we'll focus on the ones in the control panel."

"I've never seen lights there."

"You've seen Jack work there. You just didn't know what he was doing."

She showed me when we were in the hanger after using an interface in the office nearby to unlock the saucer door and deploy the ramp. "Blue means satisfactorily completed. Red is getting started. The rest are stages of implementation and there are as many stages as there are colors."

"Hundreds?"

"More like thousands." My heart sank at the enormity of the task. "Don't worry. You'll be able to pilot a saucer in a minimally adequate manner very soon."

It was so totally different from what I'd expected, even after watching Jack, that I was overwhelmed. How do you fly a craft by manipulating colors? "You think I can actually do it?"

"It's a steep learning curve but the basics aren't hard. You'll get them quickly. From then on it's a matter of practice and experience and then more practice and more experience."

She paused to let that sink in. "You won't pilot a saucer by yourself for years. It's that complicated and, in a way, that easy. Just learn the colors. But there are thousands of colors. And color combinations." She pointed to the control counsel. "So, take a look. See what you see. Look for the colors."

I did as she said and knew beyond a doubt that I'd fail horribly because all I saw was a control panel. No colors. But I kept staring because I didn't want to admit defeat immediately. I wanted to give myself a few minutes before declaring myself a failure and asking to go home.

Then I saw a faint change in the panel. A change from pure white to something a bit different though the color was so subtle and so deep in the panel that I could understand why I'd not seen it when Jack piloted the saucer. It was only visible to someone directly over it. But was this what Mazie wanted me to see?

Then something additional happened. A pink haze flashed across the screen and was gone. I blinked and wondered if it was a mirage. Then it happened again, deeper pink this time and it stayed longer. Over my shoulder Mazie said, "Good work. You're getting a response."

"It's not red like you said it should be. It's not much of a color at all."

"Put your hand over the panel and see what happens."

"What should I expect? I want to be prepared."

"I don't know exactly because everyone is different. Your hand above the panel blocks the light and that starts the flight sequence. People are so different that the blocking effect varies according to who's doing it. We've learned to keep away from the panel except when we want the saucer to do something because once it gets used to you, it becomes almost touchy."

"It sounds to me like the whole things is based on guesswork."

"It started out that way but I promise that someday you'll tell it what to do and you won't know precisely how you're doing what you do but the lights will blink and the saucer will respond and you'll be confident in your ability to control it. Because you'll just know what it will do next. It's intuitive."

She inspected the control panel and nodded approvingly as the pink darkened to light red. "Jack is good. He can make the saucer sit up and do tricks no one else can do and I doubt he can tell you what he's doing. It's that instinctive." I told her about the previous evening's ride. "That's typical of Jack. He's good, possibly the best pilot in the place."

I had to ask. "Then why isn't he teaching me?"

"Because he's a lousy teacher. You'd scream in frustration if he tried to teach you anything. Or he'd throw you across the room." The control panel was true red. Mazie pointed. "It's happening. Bright red means it's ready for your orders." I pulled my hand back in sheer terror and Mazie replaced my hands over the panel with her own and the red changed to scarlet and then to yellow. Her expression was the same as Jacks before the acrobatics. "Let's take this thing out and see what she can do." She turned to me. "What you can make her do."

CHAPTER THIRTEEN

"TAKE HER OUT." Mazie stood with her arms folded, waiting for me to do something.

"I don't know how to steer it. I'll crash it for sure."

"I'll be with you. You won't crash."

I stared helplessly at the control panel with red colors pulsating deep in the interior. "I don't even know how to get it out of the hanger."

"Move your hands the way you want the saucer to move."

"Up?"

"Yes, but not too far. An inch and see what happens." I did as she said and the saucer rose slightly. I remembered Jack doing the same thing but all I'd been aware of was his hands moving over the control panel. Now I knew what he'd been doing. I tried another inch and the saucer rose higher.

Mazie was beside me, watching and nodding approval. "Now go horizontal towards the hatch." I did so very slowly and slowly the saucer moved towards the hatch that opened as we approached. "Remember to drop into the water when we get that far." I did as she said, and the saucer responded.

"I can do it. I can pilot a flying saucer."

Laughter was in her voice. "I told you the basic stuff is easy. You'll do just fine for now but don't get too cocky. None of us knows everything there is to know about flying saucers. That's why Thom keeps working on them, learning more and more every day but each thing he learns shows how much more there is to be figured out."

We moved through the ocean and then rose into the air, and I did it with Mazie watching and standing by in case I messed up. But I didn't mess up and we went for a gentle ride over Antarctica. Mazie pointed to a holographic map I'd not noticed on one side of the control panel. "It's Antarctica. We avoid places with people and that's getting to be more all the time. So let's go high."

I did as she said and we spent the rest of the day with me learning how to fly and she was right, it was easy. I had to remind myself not to be cocky. Then we returned to the facility, and she said that was enough for one day. As I left the hanger, I looked ahead to several hours before night. I was high from the day's lesson and antsy. I didn't know what do with myself.

I went to the viewing room and looked out over the Antarctic Ocean and let my mind go blank until I heard a soft meowing and turned to see Callie meandering about the room. Where Callie was, I knew I'd find Jack. I looked around and, sure enough, he came out of the elevator after her and after making sure the door was shut so she couldn't get anywhere without him he came to me.

"I thought I'd find you here."

"Because you know me."

"I'm learning." He hooked his fingers in his belt

and looked at me, top to bottom and back. No expression except in his eyes and they were smiling.

"I'm glad you're here." I found myself smiling in return.

We let the silence drop around us like a cloak as we watched ice blue waves roll endlessly beyond the windows, breaking against the frozen white land. It was beautiful and cold, and I shivered and Jack stepped closer and wrapped me in his arms. "I'll keep you warm."

I waited for what would come next. More hugging. Kissing. Whatever. It didn't happen even though I wished it would. I liked the feel of him and thought maybe this was the beginning of his 'hitting on me' as he'd said he would.

I leaned back against his chest anyway and kind of wiggled to a more comfortable spot. Then I waited to see if he'd do more and wanted to purr like Callie when he did, which showed just how much I did, indeed, enjoy that attention but I decided things were too slow and turned in his embrace and put my arms around his neck. I felt his surprise at my action followed almost instantly by his arms tightening around me and for a time we forgot the Antarctic scenery because we were too busy with each other.

Good. Things were progressing nicely in both my professional and personal life.

The viewing room became our place after that, where we went each day after my lessons with Mazie, at least when he wasn't gone on patrol. But after that first time, all we did was talk. I never knew why he didn't make moves on me again but he didn't. I was puzzled but followed his lead, which meant absolutely nothing happened.

Which, in a way, was just as well and he possibly knew it. Learning to pilot a flying saucer was an awesome thing. Mazie had said Jack was one of the best pilots Thom had, possibly the best and I had a million questions, and he was the perfect person to answer them. Sexual attraction could wait. Not too long, I hoped, but at the moment I wanted to learn all I could about flying saucers.

As Mazie had said, learning the basics was easy. Play the lights like a kid plays a piano, I was told, and giving the saucer orders was as simple as playing Happy Birthday. I knew I'd never be done learning because she'd made sure I knew that but I began to understand what she meant when she said the pilots had no problem placing both their faith and their lives in the hands of the saucers even though they didn't know everything about them.

Long before I expected, Mazie said I was ready for the last lesson. "We go to the moon tomorrow."

"You mean the real moon or was that just a figure of speech?"

"I mean tomorrow we go to the real moon where we'll have to be careful not to be seen by any prying telescopes or probes or robots exploring the surface and reporting back everything they see."

"So, we'll go to the back side?"

"Yes, and even then we'll have to be on the lookout for robots prowling the surface though we do have their coordinates in our computers and we watch them pretty closely. Thom installed computers in the saucers for that and other reasons."

Her words caught my attention. The woman was a

walking dictionary. Everything she said had meaning. "What are the 'other' reasons?"

"Communication with the facility though we are very careful with every type of communication. Don't want anyone listening to know what we're doing. Other than that, locating meteors are the second most important thing." She shuddered. "Don't want them plowing into us. Computers track the worst ones, and the saucers automatically avoid them but we are always on the alert anyway."

"I thought saucers are impervious to collisions because they are a universe inside of a universe." The guided missiles hadn't even pitted the side of the saucer when Jack and I were on our way to the facility and that saucer had been barely functional. Surely a fully functional saucer would be safe. On the other hand, that saucer had plowed into a mountain.

"They should be impervious but space is large and pretty much unknown. Best to be prepared for the unknowable than to find out later we weren't careful enough."

"Has anyone ever had a serious problem?"

"No." She thought over her answer and added, "Not yet." Then she told me to enjoy the rest of the day and be in the hanger bright and early the next morning. "Bright and early being metaphoric because in a windowless facility we can't truly experience either bright or early."

I felt actual chills when I guided the saucer into the ocean and then up into the sky at what would have been dawn at home and was still dark in Antarctica. The chills turned icy as we left the atmosphere and plowed through near earth orbit and then kept going into space itself. The moon was small in the sky but grew larger faster than seemed possible.

I was terrified and Mazie sensed my fear. "Just keep doing what you're doing. We'll stay far enough above the moon's surface to not have to worry about mountains so it'll be just like flying above the earth." I reminded her that we'd stayed pretty high above the earth in my previous lessons in order not to be seen instead of not to plow into anything. "That is true and someday you'll practice flying low but for now higher is safer and just going around the moon is enough. I want to give you a feel for being in space."

The sky was black. Stars were dots. The sun was bright on one side of the moon while the other side was dark but not so dark that we couldn't make out features on the surface. As we traversed the back side, I found myself wanting to go lower to better see what that surface was like but I also wanted to stay alive so I probably stayed farther out than necessary. But all the time Mazie said nothing, just kept nodding to herself as we circumnavigated the moon a dozen times.

Then we went home, and I was presented with a cake topped by a tiny figure of Atlas with the world on his shoulders because I'd just become a vetted member of the Atlas Project. A kind of graduation ceremony the Patrol did with all new members.

I learned the Project actually had a motto. Two mottos. "To Grow And Learn" and "To Explore And Protect." I felt those words from my head to my toes and knew I'd won the brass ring and wished I could call my family and brag a bit.

But I had to be satisfied with a very large slice of cake and the best wishes of those Patrol members that happened to be around when Mazie and I entered the kitchen after I landed the saucer perfectly and lined it up precisely in its place in the hanger.

Jack was there. So was Thom and several others whose names I was slowly learning. There was Brock, older than Mazie, with gray hair and lines around his eyes who'd been with Thom from the beginning who said it was about time Mazie was free from her tutoring duties so they could go on patrol again. And a couple more guys named Randy and Gene respectively and a middle-aged woman named Gina who looked kind of like Gene. Siblings? Twins? I'd know eventually because we were now members of the same special and very secret organization. The thought made me want to sing.

That was the day I learned that no member of the Patrol ever went beyond Earth's atmosphere alone and that Mazie was a brilliant geologist who'd found some spectacular ore deposits on a handful of asteroids that had most likely been one large asteroid at one time that had stayed close together after something tore it apart. She'd been with Brock at the time.

Watching Brock and Mazie interact, I decided they made a good team. I'd ask Jack later if they were romantically linked as well. It was impossible to tell by watching because they were all business and enjoying cake and ice cream as if it was a rare occasion. Which, I learned later, was because the Atlas Project consisted of dozens of people instead of thousands or even hundreds so graduations were rare.

"You've survived your initial lessons," Mazie said with a gentle smile as she stuffed a third slice of cake in her mouth. I'd not known the hard-as-nails pilot was capable of gentleness until then. "But there will be a million more lessons. You'll never stop learning. Your first patrol will be a normal patrol but it will also be Phase Two of your education."

"Why not learn everything before going on patrol?"

"Because then you'd never go anywhere and because we believe in on-the-job training. You'll remember best by doing what you're learning, and you'll be with another patrol member who will teach and supervise and advise you every step of the way."

When the cake was gone and the patrol members had left the room, Thom, Jack and I remained. Thom's feet rested on a chair as he considered me thoughtfully. "You know how to fly a saucer and according to Mazie, you're ready for action so it's time to put you to work." Chills went along my spine. This was it. The day I'd learn what I was to do as a member of the Atlas Project.

He leaned closer. "I want to learn more about the ore deposits Mazie found in the asteroid belt. She and Brock are headed farther out to look for still more such treasures but I need someone to learn more about those particular asteroids. Measurements. Drilling down to see how deep the deposits go. What miners can expect when they reach it. What to watch out for. And so on."

I waited silently for the rest of his speech. I was so excited I had to remind myself to breathe. "You and Jack will make the perfect pair to double-check what Mazie says is out there."

"I'll be with Jack?"

"You two have a history. You know one another. You've flown together. It's an easy decision and we'll see how well you work together when you have an actual job to do." He dropped his legs to the floor, heaved himself out of his chair, and left.

Jack studied me. "Want to head up to the observation room?"

"Of course." It was where we'd gone every other day after that day's lesson. Why not now?

The observation room was deserted. When we stepped out of the elevator, Jack looked a question at me and, seeing my answer, locked it. "We don't need company. Today is just for you."

Every time we'd been there during my lessons, I'd had questions and he'd answered them competently and patiently. I had no questions that day. Instead, I stared out at the cold landscape and thought about Jack and me and the mission we'd been given. He came up behind me and I didn't turn, didn't acknowledge him in any way but we were so synched to each other that he knew I was aware of him.

Had Thom noticed that about us when we were together? Was that why he paired us? I didn't know, just knew that it felt right being there with Jack and that it felt even better when his lips found my neck and even better when I turned towards him even though those gentle kisses weren't enough for everything I was feeling right then. I was ready to burst with the accomplishment of becoming a saucer pilot, the pride of being a member of the Atlas Project, and the feel of Jack's very male body against my own.

CHAPTER FOURTEEN

I THOUGHT WE'D leave on patrol the next morning. I was wrong.

"First we learn everything Mazie figured out about the asteroids and the ore that she says is there."

"Is there any doubt and why do we have to learn what she already knows?'

"Mazie is the best but we aren't so we need to learn whatever we can stuff into our heads about ore and the particular cluster of asteroids we'll be checking out."

"How long will that take?"

Jack shrugged. "As long as it takes. Time here works differently than in most businesses. We aren't so much concerned with getting something done is a specific time span as we are about doing it right and returning home alive and healthy."

So, we learned about ore and asteroids. The ore in question turned out to be iron. "To make hammers and other tools," I said.

"And car engines," Jack added.

"And so much more." Mazie named half a dozen industries that used iron and she could have continued for a long time. "When the iron content of these asteroids becomes known there'll be a stampede and we've got to get ahead of it. We need to know the extent of the ore they hold and whether those asteroids are unique or merely three among many." Then she added, "Plus, if there's iron ore, there could be other ores also and the total could be worth several fortunes."

We also learned about asteroids and the asteroid belt. That is, I learned about those things. Jack already was something of an expert, having made numerous trips there. Patrols, they called their trips around the Solar System, but they didn't resemble the kind of patrols law enforcement made.

No need to protect against criminals in a place that was deserted so the patrols were more exploratory in nature and hugely important for the future of space exploration. When humanity moved beyond Earth, the patrol would be waiting.

Two weeks later we knew enough about iron, iron ore mining, and asteroids to leave Earth. Two weeks of reading and watching videos during the day and gazing at ice flows and the Antarctic Ocean from the observation room when the lessons were done though usually it was so dark by then that there was little to see. We didn't mind. We were there, we knew what the outside world was like, and it was a quiet place to relax.

It was also a place to talk about something other than iron ore and asteroids. One time as the quiet of the place seeped through us and took away some of the strain of the day's lessons, I said in a low voice because I didn't want to interrupt that comfortable vibe, "I didn't expect to be paired with you."

"I was pretty sure we'd work together."

"What made you think that?"

"The fact that I drove Thom crazy by insisting I be paired with you until he finally gave in and agreed. I told him how well we'd work together, and I told him that over and over and over again until I thought he'd physically throw me out into the Antarctic and lock the door so I couldn't return and harass him some more."

"You did that?"

"I did indeed, and it worked. We are a team and will remain one permanently if I have any say in the matter."

"Oh." Not much of a reply but the one word was all I could manage as my imagination went into overdrive about what might happen on the patrol when we'd be alone together for weeks.

It was too dark out to see much so after a few minutes of staring at nothing through the windows we'd given up and found a comfortable couch. We'd just arrived, we didn't want to leave, and we were both too antsy about the coming patrol to think of anything else. We needed that place and time to relax.

"You do know we're going to be alone together for the entire patrol," Jack said, changing the topic of conversation but he was now talking about the same thing I'd been thinking and imagining. His voice had deepened and taken on a different, new tone.

"It has occurred to me."

"And you do know that's going to be hard." He amended that. "I don't know about you but it'll be hard for me."

"You're the one who wanted me for a partner."

"True. I did want you as a partner and I do want you and I believe I always will." That baritone sent shivers through me as he sighed, sounding pretty much like Romeo watching Juliet on her balcony. Or so I hoped. "But that won't make life any easier on our first patrol together."

What was he getting at? "You expect it will get easier over time?"

"Hopefully."

That deep tone of voice suddenly seemed so comical that I laughed as he said, ruefully, "Laugh if you will, I've got a sort of plan for the future but it's going to be a bumpy road getting from the here and now to the fruition of the plan."

"What is the end result?" As if I didn't know. But in truth he'd not said so I truly didn't know what he wanted out of our relationship. If we had a relationship. I hoped we did but suddenly, sitting there in the observation room, I wasn't even sure about that.

His brow creased as he said darkly, "You'll find out. At least you will if it turns out as I hope." Then he added, "And just so you know, I'm not the choirboy type but I'm sitting here looking like one while sitting on my hands instead of placing them where I'd like to."

"Which is where exactly?" I had to remind myself to breathe.

He sighed a great sigh. "You asked. If you didn't ask, I'd keep sitting here quietly and passively. But you asked so I'll answer." And so slowly that I could retreat at any moment if I chose to do so, he reached for me.

I, of course, made no move to prevent myself being pulled towards him even as I wondered how long we'd be in the asteroid belt. My imagination added a few details I'd not thought of before about what might happen while we were there. Then reality intruded on my thoughts as I wondered whether he'd still want to be with me when we came back or whether he'd be begging for a different partner. Could go either way.

We stayed in the observation room far longer than we should have considering a good night's sleep was advisable before leaving Earth, but we were too busy learning about each other to notice the time or think of much of anything beyond ourselves.

When we finally went to our rooms Jack hesitated at my door. He wanted to join me but we were facing weeks alone together. If things didn't work out, those weeks could go very badly if we started something now that we'd regret. An odd thought but as we stood there and did nothing it settled in my mind, and I couldn't shove it away.

So, I pretended not to notice what he wanted. Of course, he knew what I was doing but instead of saying anything he gave me a half salute and went across the hall to his own room and his waiting kitten.

We both slept late the next morning. Thom's eyebrows rose when we entered the kitchen for a late breakfast. "Couple of sleepyheads," was all he said though he examined us closely. Evidently satisfied with what he saw he proceeded to give us a rundown on what preparations had been made for our patrol.

"More provisions than usual because we don't want you to have to return to the facility for more if what you find requires further investigation. One of the largest saucers, of course, to accommodate all those provisions and the equipment you'll need. Take as long as the job requires. Stay as long as it takes. Do the job right."

I'd never been in a large saucer. It was awesome and huge, with concentric circles for storage and living and others that could have been medical or laboratories with the innermost raised circle being where the control panel was located with windows all around. But the controls were exactly the same in this huge saucer as in the smaller ones I was now familiar with.

"Take it out," Jack said quietly after Thom left and the ramp retracted, and the door was closed. "Get us out of here, Elena."

"Me?" My eyes must have gone wide. "It's huge. I've never flown one so large. It'll be like trying to control a flying elephant."

"A very well-trained elephant that will do whatever you tell it to do." He folded his arms and didn't move an inch towards the control panel, and it dawned on me that this was surely what all new pilots were instructed to do once they'd finished their basic education. Fly the biggest saucer in the place to learn what it was like and prove to themselves that they could do it.

So I went to the control panel and looked deep into it until the colors came. A faint blush that grew deeper and deeper until it was pink and then red and I could use my hands to tell it what to do. As I took it out of the hanger and across the landing strip and into the ocean, I felt once more that flying a saucer was more akin to being the conductor of an orchestra than the pilot of a flying craft.

We got through the water with no major problems and into the air but I didn't breathe a sigh of relief until we were high above the clouds where the huge size of the saucer was not a problem and no one below could see our progress or get in our way. Then I turned to Jack, and he took over because, after all, he knew the way to the asteroid belt and I didn't. He'd been there, I'd only been to the moon.

We moved out of Earth's orbit and swung around the moon but after that time seemed to stop. "Are we going slower than when we started this trip or is it my imagination?"

"You are right. We slowed down. We're not likely to be spotted now so we don't have to get away from nosy telescopes quickly. And there's no hurry."

"So we can go faster if we choose?"

"Absolutely." Something about his expression said he'd love to show me just how fast we could go and the speed would be mind-blowing. But he kept the saucer slow and steady.

"Why don't we speed up a bit? We're in space. That's what spaceships do, isn't it? Go fast?"

"Thom long ago decided not to push these craft when we are away from Earth's orbit because if we overdo anything and cause a malfunction it could be a dicey situation until help arrives and we might not survive. We don't know everything about them. So we don't take chances. Ever."

"Has anyone ever needed help?"

"No, they haven't and hopefully no one ever will because we are very careful. But it does make for a rather long and somewhat boring journey." He checked that holographic map of the solar system hanging in the air near the control panel and plotted a course that would have us pass through Mars' orbit and then straight to the cluster of asteroids Mazie had discovered.

He used his hands to pull the map until it was over the console and a flash of light indicated the two had connected. "We're on automatic pilot now." He left the console and came to where I was watching the stars against the blackness of space with Callie on my shoulder because of course she came with us. She was a veteran of many such patrols.

As soon as Jack got close enough, she jumped from my shoulder to his and I realized that the kitten knew when her guy was working and shouldn't be bothered but she also knew when it was okay to meow for attention, such as right then and Callie's look invited me to join them.

The kitten mewed her contentment so I went close to join them. Jack wrapped me in warmth, and it felt so good that I wanted to stay that way forever, watching the blackness of space filled with unwinking stars so far away they appeared static.

It would take a week to reach Mars at our reduced speed and more days, maybe weeks, to reach the asteroid belt, then possibly still more days to find the cluster of iron ore asteroids Mazie had mapped. We knew they'd look no different from the thousands of other asteroids we'd thread through and that only when we checked the pictures Mazie had taken against the reality of the belt and found a match, would we know for sure we'd arrived.

"What then?"

"Then we land on the largest one and see what it's like."

"How do we do that?"

"We go for a walk and take some equipment with us."

My mouth dropped in shock. "There's no atmosphere not to mention not much gravity."

"We wear space suits and clip ourselves to tethers."

"We have space suits?"

"We do indeed, and Thom made sure we have the best available in all sizes thanks to spreading a lot of money around the space industry. We brought one for me and one that will fit you perfectly even if you are the smallest member of the Atlas Project. And a couple extras for each of us."

He led the way to one of the outer concentric circles and showed me a suit locker I'd not known existed. "Before we go outside there will be plenty of time to practice getting into and out of your suit and to learn about how it works, not to mention learning how to operate the tethers."

"Why didn't we do that before we left the facility?"

"Because, as Mazie said, we believe in on-the-job training. Besides, this gives us something to do during the long, boring trip to the asteroid belt."

"More classes," I said resignedly.

"More classes indeed." He chuckled. "You were told we never stop learning in this business and now you know how life-long learning works."

"And why my first classes didn't last long. Because they were introductory in nature."

"Phase Two of your education begins with space suits."

CHAPTER FIFTEEN

I'D EXPECTED TO spend the time between planets learning about Jack while he learned about me. After all, when we were in the woods behind my house, he'd said he'd be hitting on me but the majority of the time in the observation room when we were alone together had been spent talking. So, I'd expected we'd make up for lost time on the patrol.

But nothing happened during that long boring time between planets. In fact, he very carefully avoided me. Why?

I worried about the lack of anything happening. I obsessed. I stared into the mirror in my tiny room. Was something wrong with me? Had he changed his mind now that we actually worked together? Did he regret those fateful wonderful words? Did he now think he'd made a mistake asking for us to be together?

Were those few chaste kisses we'd shared so far his way of letting me down gently? Had a relationship that had started hot and promising turned into a boring nothing?

It was beginning to look that way.

But learning about space suits was interesting. Not interesting enough to make me believe things were going well but it did take my mind off being jilted.

The main thing I learned about space suits was that they were large, cumbersome and difficult to put on and take off. Their saving grace was that in space there's little to no gravity so it would be possible to do things while wearing them that would have been impossible while wearing them on Earth.

Or so Jack said. With normal gravity in the saucer, it was impossible to try them out. We helped each other into and out of the suits until I knew how they worked. "Now put it on by yourself. Then take it off without my help."

"Why? There are two of us and we work well together." Jack wasn't a horrible teacher as Mazie had said. Not completely horrible anyway. Infuriating maybe, but that was all.

"Out of an abundance of caution you should be able to do everything yourself. Not just space suits, you should know and be able to do absolutely everything without help."

"I don't know everything about flying saucers but I'm in one right now and I've been told I'm a working part of the crew so that fact invalidates what you just said."

"Saucers are the single exception to the rule. If you waited until you knew everything about them, you'd never go anywhere. None of us would. They are weird. But there are no other exceptions and space suits are important. So, show me you understand how they function."

I wanted to stick out my tongue at him. Instead, I gave the space suit a look of pure hatred and put the darn thing on. Then I took it off. I was amazed. "I actually did it."

"And now you know you can do it alone if needed."

"We're done with Phase Two?"

"We will be done after you practice many, many more times and learn a few more things."

I stared at his implacable self and decided maybe Mazie was right after all. He was a lousy teacher. "How many more times?"

"Until I say you can quit." I did stick my tongue out at him then, but it had no effect other than to make his eyes light up with enjoyment at my misery, after which I put the suit on and took it off numerous times. Enough times that I could do it in my sleep and in the dark.

By the time we passed Mars' orbit Jack decided I knew how to put on my spacesuit. I looked for Mars eagerly but it wasn't there at the time so we didn't see it. A disappointment that I forgot when we reached our destination. The asteroid belt. Except it didn't look like much. It looked empty.

"Asteroids aren't close together," Jack said, answering my question before I asked. "Not like you'd expect. Which is good. No problem navigating to the ones we are interested in."

"Will those also be far from each other?"

"Not according to Mazie, which is why we think what's now a cluster of three was originally one asteroid that somehow broke into pieces."

"Mazie knows her business."

"It'll be nice to validate her findings." Jack hovered over the control panel, glancing from the panel to the holographic map above it and back as the saucer slowed. Not that I could feel any difference but I'd learned enough about saucers to know when we were reaching the end of our journey. Blue slowly became the dominant color. "We should see them shortly."

And then we did, both in the holographic display and the real asteroids beyond the windows. "Dark," Jack said unnecessarily. "They are almost black and are hard to see so they possibly haven't been discovered yet except by Mazie."

One of the asteroids was large. It was bisected by a rocky zigzag ridge down the middle but other than that it had a fairly regular surface. It would be easy to land on. I looked at the locker. Anticipation began to build. "Have you ever walked on a planet or an asteroid?"

"Yes."

"What's it like?"

He waved the hologram to one side and gave me his full attention. "Odd. It's quite odd but I think you'll like it and this mission requires that the two of us be outside. I'll take ore samples and you'll monitor the tether." He bit his lip, thinking. "But remember to never unclip yourself from your tether. Not ever."

Which had been the part of the Phase Two lesson that we'd got to after leaving the Mars orbit and before we reached the asteroid belt. Tethers and the dangers of little to no gravity. I'd paid close attention because drifting into space never to return wasn't appealing. Learning how to stay alive even superseded wondering whether I was being jilted though Jack's lack of attention was making it more and more clear that I was.

We made careful notes of each asteroid's position. Jack's face was carefully blank. "I'll go out first and check to make sure the asteroid is solid enough to be safe."

"Are you saying it might not be?"

"You stay here while I check it out."

"Oh no you don't! I refuse to be stuck inside because you've suddenly decided to be a protective male."

"I'm not that. I might need you in here."

I almost laughed. "You need me outside. You said so less than a minute ago."

He raked a hand through his hair, frowned in frustration, and finally accepted the truth. "We do need the tethers, and someone has to watch them."

"I promise to take care of you, Jack." I gave him a smile that was sweet enough to kill after which his face became the perfect picture of the male of the species torn between wanting to take care of the nearest female, wanting to throttle me, and appreciating that I'd got around his excuse and would soon be walking on the surface of an unknown asteroid millions of miles from Earth. His expression also acknowledged that I was an essential part of the team. That last made me burst with pride even as I decided maybe I hated him as well as wanting him to wrap me in his embrace.

After donning our space suits, we left the saucer, which involved snapping the ends of the tethers to our suits and the other ends to the innermost wall of the airlock. Only when our work was done, and we'd reeled ourselves back into the airlock and shut the door would we unsnap the tethers and remove our suits because then we'd be safe and secure as the airlock filled with air. It was a safe system. Secure. Efficient. Foolproof.

Jack was right about walking on an asteroid. It was odd and strangely enjoyable. I wanted to hop, step, and jump around but we had work to do so I set the wish aside and focused on paying out Jack's tether as he snapped pictures of iron ore veins threaded through the rocky surface and took samples every few yards, placing them in a bag brought for that purpose.

All in all, everything went well.

Until it didn't.

We never knew why it happened. It could have been the added mass of the saucer. Or our moving around. Or perhaps it was simply time for it to happen. After all, it had happened before. What had once been one asteroid was three when we arrived. So, it could have just been bad timing that Jack was at the end of his tether when the asteroid we were on broke in half.

I was on the part with the saucer. Jack was on the other part. The part that went flying. He'd have been thrown into space if he wasn't connected to the tether.

The tether held for a few moments. But it wasn't strong enough. It whipsawed one way and then another, throwing him back and forth as I watched in horror as his body contorted into shapes no human could do naturally.

Then the worst happened. The tether snapped and Jack began to float away. The only good thing was that the whipsaw motion had lessened so he moved slowly. Slowly enough for me to catch him.

I started towards him, hopping, running, jumping as fast as my suit would allow. But I couldn't reach him. My tether wasn't long enough for me to grab him, and he didn't reach for me. Didn't look at me. Didn't turn towards me. Didn't do anything except float, turning in lazy circles in the black of space just beyond reach.

Was he alive? I couldn't know. But I chose to believe he was.

Before I could tell myself not to do anything foolish, I unclipped my tether and used the oxygen in my tank to jet towards him. I prayed he'd see and reach out to me. That he'd help me rescue him. But he did nothing. Saw nothing. Just rolled over and over in slow motion and began to ever so slowly float away.

I gave another jet of oxygen and prayed I'd not run out before I could return to the saucer. If I could return. If Jack and I both didn't end up floating forever in space.

I reached him. Grabbed him, turned him towards me, and saw that he was unconscious. Dead? I refused to consider the possibility. But I had to get him back to the saucer to know how bad things were.

How to do that? There were two of us so there was more bulk to move, and my oxygen was just about used up. But Jack's wasn't. I found his control valve and used his oxygen to jet us towards the saucer as I wrapped my free arm and both of my legs around him to hold us together. I prayed we'd reach the saucer or at least the tether I'd left floating freely. If I was lucky, I could grab it.

I almost missed the tether. I would have if we hadn't run into it and gotten tangled. But even with the lifeline in my grasp it took precious moments to untangle us, then even more to clip the tether to Jack's suit and still more to jerk the tether three times to signal the saucer to haul us back. I held onto Jack hard as the tether responded. Even so I was almost thrown.

But I managed to keep us both together and we moved towards the saucer. But we didn't move fast enough, which I realized when a beeping sound told me I was about to run out of oxygen. If we couldn't get back into the saucer so I could close the hatch and oxygen could flood the chamber before I lost consciousness we'd both die.

The tether was slow. I felt myself losing consciousness. Then something happened. We speeded up. I managed to see what was happening even as the darkness began swirling around me that would end in my losing consciousness. The tether had pulled us close enough to the saucer for the tractor beam to take over. It pulled us quickly to the open hatch. I managed to get us both inside and close the door and pull both my helmet and Jack's off. Then I simply lay back and cried in relief.

But there still wasn't enough oxygen in the airlock to enable us to breathe. Everything went black.

CHAPTER SIXTEEN

I REGAINED CONSCIOUSNESS on the floor of the airlock. It took precious seconds to remember what had happened. Then I rolled over enough to get a look at Jack. He didn't look good. He was still unconscious. A trickle of blood seeped through his lips. And he was still. So still. He didn't move at all, and his breathing was shallow and irregular. As if it would stop any moment.

But he was alive, and I'd better do something to keep him that way. But what? I wasn't a doctor, I knew nothing about injuries and it was obvious they were bad. I tore off my suit and clumsily removed his. I opened the airlock to the inside of the saucer and tried to think what to do. How to get him inside without breaking any more of his poor body than was already broken.

I felt helpless. Hurting. Angry that this had happened. Furious. And I couldn't do anything because I was inside a flying saucer. A thing. An inanimate object that knew nothing and did nothing beyond what it had been programmed to do.

But through my anger, a memory surfaced. I remembered the first time I'd been in a flying saucer.

Its programming must have been extensive because that saucer had repaired itself. I'd seen it happen on the mountain when I climbed through a hole that grew smaller as I watched.

There was no place in the asteroid belt where Jack could be fixed but the saucer hadn't had to worry about that because it could repair itself and it could do so anywhere. Which wasn't fair. Jack's life blood was seeping away, his breathing was growing fainter and it would soon stop altogether.

We weren't where he could be cared for. I couldn't help him. I wanted to cry. Instead, I screamed in frustration. "Saucer!" I yelled as loudly as I was able even though it wouldn't help Jack. I yelled because I was furious with it for having been fixed when Jack couldn't be. "You fixed yourself!" I stared at the walls and screamed louder. "Now fix Jack!"

Then I caught my breath and went totally silent because as soon as the words were spoken colors began to appear. First red, as always happened because red was the beginning color. Then the red fragmented into more colors than I knew existed. As happened every time the saucer flew.

But this time those colors didn't remain in the control panel or on the wall or any other place that was part of the saucer itself. Instead, they moved through the air until they hovered over Jack.

As I watched in total awe some of the colors seemed to enter Jack's body while others continued to hover over him. Was it answering my scream? Protecting him? Checking on his injuries? Whatever they were doing, they encased him in a rainbow of -- something. Warmth? Safety?

I didn't know, just that watching it happen made me stop breathing as a faint thread of hope began somewhere in my middle and curled through me. I didn't know what was happening but something was. Something better than watching him die.

I didn't speak. I hardly breathed because if the saucer was doing what that faint ray of hope said it was doing then the best thing I could do was not interfere. But doing nothing was hard. I wanted to say something. To encourage it. To ask if it was truly doing what I hoped. But I forced myself to remain curled on the floor of the airlock.

I don't know how long I remained that way or how long the colors encased Jack in that beautiful rainbow. It could have been minutes. Maybe an hour. But I was thrust out of my reverie by the airlock door opening. Not the door to the inner part of the saucer itself – that was already open – but the door to space.

I gasped. We'd die with the door open to the vacuum of space. I wanted to scream once more because I'd been wrong all along. The saucer wasn't saving Jack. It was killing us both.

Except the air in the room didn't whoosh out to space and leave us to gasp our last breaths. Instead, nothing happened. It was as if the door had opened onto the landing strip of the facility instead of to space.

Then the colors moved again, changing somehow, swirling faster and faster around Jack. It was then I realized we weren't in space at all. While I'd been sitting in agony watching the lights and hoping they were saving Jack's life the saucer had taken off on its own and flown us to someplace unknown. I looked through the open hatch to see where we were and saw that we were in the landing strip in the facility.

How had we gotten there so quickly? It didn't make sense because no matter how long I'd sat numbly beside Jack it hadn't been long enough to travel from the asteroid belt to Earth.

But then I stopped trying to figure out where we were because the lights around Jack changed. They moved until they were beneath him. They wove themselves into a basket that gently, slowly, without hurting him at all, raised him into the air. Then they floated him through the open hatch, down the ramp, and into the facility itself.

I scrambled to my feet and followed. As I ran down the ramp, I realized this wasn't the facility after all though it was similar in many respects. The landing strip was the same but smaller, there was no glassed-in office for Thom, and we hadn't come through the ocean.

The lights carried Jack ever so gently to a room I'd not seen in the facility on Earth. It was obviously medical in nature. A bed unfolded from the wall and Jack was floated onto it just as gently as he'd been moved. More lights came out of the wall and moved over his body only this time there were so many lights of so many colors that I realized what I'd seen so far was merely a fraction of what the saucer could produce.

The saucer was indeed healing Jack. At the very least it was trying to keep him alive. That was the only explanation I could come up with and I gave thanks that in my agony I'd screamed for the saucer to save Jack and it was following my order.

I wanted to ask the colors what his chances were. But if I asked and they replied in a show of colors I wouldn't know what they were saying so I remained silent and simply watched as the colors changed and morphed until they appeared solid. Then they *were* solid and carrying what must have been life-saving medicines into Jack's body.

I hoped and prayed that was truly what I was seeing happen as I bit my tongue and kept watching. Then I knew for a certainty that the colors were indeed healing him because as time passed the lights grew fewer and fewer until the only color left was gold. Gold? Blue always meant the conclusion of a successful incident. Just like when flying. Red to begin a project and blue at the finish. But this was gold. Was that good or bad?

The golden haze grew brighter around Jack, and I couldn't stay away any longer. I approached him on that pristine white bed. Whatever the colors had done, they were finished, at least for the time being. I examined him from top to bottom and saw that his breathing was deep and even. The rhythm of life instead of the brink of death. The saucer had saved his life. I knew that as profoundly as I knew myself.

The colors had somehow removed Jack's bloody clothes and replaced them with what looked like soft white blankets, all done while swirling about him and keeping him alive. Now he needed sleep. I knew that because it's what all people who have been badly injured need. And I could finally get out of my own torn and dirty clothes and come to grips with what had just happened. What miracle had been performed before my eyes.

I stared and tried to think what to do next. I couldn't think of anything because I didn't know what was happening. I finally, reluctantly, accepted that perhaps I should deal with myself and after I was human again with whatever had happened.

I trudged back through the strange facility to the saucer because it contained my things. My clothes, soap, shampoo, and everything else I needed for day-to-day life and right then I found myself looking forward to the normalcy of those everyday things. I told myself over and over that Jack was in as good a place as was possible considering what he'd been through. I could think beyond him. I could consider myself and I should. Besides, there was nothing else I could do. I had to trust the colors so I closed my eyes, gave a short prayer, and took a shower.

I made myself a sandwich, brushed my hair until I had to stop because, though the motion made it possible for me to not think and I wanted that blankness, life beckoned and needed to be acknowledged. I must keep going. I must figure out what to do next in this totally bizarre experience and that would take some serious thinking.

I was clean and nourished and Callie said she'd been left alone long enough so she and I sat for a long time just letting what had happened sink in. Then I gently set the sleeping kitten down and returned to Jack's room. His hospital room, as I thought of it, because it was close to what I'd see in any hospital on Earth only with colors where there would normally be monitors and medical gadgets. It was a beautiful room. I decided I preferred colors to gadgets.

Jack was still enveloped in that golden glow. He looked so peaceful that I breathed deeply for the first time since the asteroid flew apart, tossed him into space, and broke his body.

I crept close and stared at him for a long time. And I realized something. I not only wanted his kisses now and then as in the viewing room back on Earth, I wanted him. I wanted Jack. I more than wanted him. I needed him. I needed him in my life just as he'd said he wanted me in his, only now I knew exactly how he'd felt because I felt it myself.

So why did I feel this sudden need for him just as he decided he didn't need me? It wasn't fair.

My next thoughts were totally irrational and completely honest. I decided he'd darn well better recover so I could tell him just how unfair he was being. I'd yell at him for a while first, of course, when he was conscious, for having the temerity to go and almost die on me. Then I'd change tactics. I'd politely ask if my romantic feelings would bother him too much because, after all, he'd not made any moves on me recently so obviously didn't love me.

But one-sided love is better than none, I decided as I sat there and stared at him and made peace with the rest of my life. If unrequited love was all I'd have then I'd just make it be enough. I wouldn't tell him that out loud, of course. I'd just think it. Because he'd almost died and shouldn't be yelled at too hard until he recovered somewhat. But he'd be alive and that was the most important thing for the moment. The only important thing. My feelings were inconsequential in comparison to his life, something I told myself many times as I sat there.

I'd make sure he understood that I wasn't angry, and I could do so because I'm a good liar. I'd also make him understand that I was only telling him how I felt because we'd be in close contact forever because we were both members of the Atlas Project and thus couldn't avoid seeing each other on a daily basis. But I'd let him know that I didn't want to guilt him. I'd be sure to tell him that it was fine with me if he ignored my feelings. My love for him.

Then I'd sit back and watch his confusion as he tried to figure how to deal with me for the rest of our lives. And I'd enjoy every second because I deserved it after the way he'd dumped me and then gone on to almost die.

Having decided what I'd do when he woke up, I looked around for something to sit on while I waited for that to happen, but the room was bare except for the bed and the golden haze that meant Jack was going to be okay. At least I hoped that was what it meant.

Sitting would be nice. I was tired and as I thought over what had happened in the last few hours, I figured maybe there was a way I could have a chair. The saucer had heard me before. It had done what I told it to do. Maybe it was still listening.

Maybe it always listened.

I decided to find out. "Hey, Saucer." Nothing. No indication it could hear, but I kept speaking anyway. "I'd appreciate something to sit on because I'm staying right here until I'm sure Jack is okay, and it'll get uncomfortable after a while. So, a chair would be nice. Please get me a chair. And something so I can take a nap."

It did as I asked. Colors appeared and when they dissipated a chair had folded out of the wall and was beside Jack's bed and a second bed was on his other side, only this one was a normal bed for someone to sleep in instead of a hospital type such as Jack's.

"Thank you, Saucer," I said, remembering my manners because it definitely understood what I was saying, and it might be waiting for my thanks. Maybe it understood the subtleties of human interactions and expected good manners. Even if it didn't, it's always smart to stay on the good side of anything imbued with superpowers and good manners are a good start.

I dropped into the surprisingly comfortable chair with a sigh of relief and stared at Jack until I found myself nodding off, partly because the chair was soft but also because I was hypnotized by that golden glow. Moments later, Callie found me, having left the saucer and followed me somehow, and climbed into my lap, curling into a calico ball and staring at Jack as if she'd rather be with him. But the lights were too intimidating. She wasn't that brave, so I'd have to do.

I looked beyond Jack to that second bed. I grabbed Callie, left the chair, crawled into it and dropped my head onto the pillow that smelled like it had been freshly laundered though I couldn't imagine how that could be. Callie curled beside me, and I pulled the blankets up to my chin and instantly fell asleep.

It had been an extremely intense day. I was exhausted. Maybe not physically but mentally I was wiped out. I slept deeply and without dreams. I was beyond dreaming. Besides, dreams couldn't begin to deal with what I'd experienced.

CHAPTER SEVENTEEN

WHEN I AWOKE, the first thing I did was check on Jack. He seemed unchanged, still breathing deeply and evenly, still encased in that golden glow that I hoped meant he was on the mend. Then, so suddenly I didn't have time to blink, colored lights came out of the wall and zipped around and through him for a few moments before disappearing back where they'd come from.

What had just happened? Had the lights given him needed medication? Or was he relapsing? Had the lights dealt with a problem if he had one? Or was he beyond hope and they were merely making him comfortable until the end came? The bottom dropped out of my stomach as I realized I'd been hoping the lights were healing him. In reality, I had no idea what was going on.

Jack slept on but I knew I wouldn't be able to sleep until I knew what those lights meant. They were now gone, having disappeared into the wall. Was that good or bad? The golden glow was what remained. What did that mean exactly? Jack slept peacefully. Did that mean anything? We he recovering or was he dying?

I was tied in emotional knots. I hugged Callie

fiercely because I had to do something, and she was handy. Not knowing what was going on couldn't continue, I informed her as she meowed angrily because I was squeezing her too hard, or I'd lose my mind. Guessing wasn't good enough.

But the only way to know what was actually happening was to communicate with the saucer. Or with the facility because both place and craft seemed to be linked. I needed to truly communicate with something in charge and get answers, not just give orders and wait to see if they'd be followed.

But how do you communicate with a bunch of lights?

I stared furiously at that golden glow as if doing so would make it tell me something. Anything. But nothing changed. Jack still slept like a baby in the middle of a pool of gold.

As I stared at that golden glow, though, I realized I did know one thing. The saucer would do what I told it to do. I stood up, cleared my throat, set Callie on the floor, and said, "Saucer, tell me how Jack is doing health-wise." Almost instantly a thousand colors lit the room, threading through each other, caroming from one side of the room to the other, and generally dancing everywhere.

The saucer had done what I wanted it to do. It told me all about Jack. I just couldn't understand what it said because I didn't speak its language. The only good thing that came from the light display was that Callie somewhat lost her fear of the lights. She batted at them. They didn't respond so they were probably okay with one small kitten. But I was nowhere closer to knowing about Jack than before.

I sat back down on that chair, thought a lot, and then grabbed Callie and petted her so hard she meowed in protest again as I thought some more. I thought harder. I thought differently. Surely there was a way for me to communicate with the lights. But how?

As soon as I thought the question, I had a potential answer. So, I stood up once more, cleared my throat again, held Callie close, and said as politely as I knew how, "Saucer, I don't understand your colored light language." I crossed my fingers that what I was about to say would make sense to it. "There are too many colors. I can't follow that many. But I can understand one or two colors. If you'll blink red three times for 'no' and yellow three times for 'yes,' when I ask a question then I'll understand your answer."

I took a couple deep breaths and continued. "Do you understand what I'm asking you to do?"

A yellow light blinked three times. I felt like cheering. We could communicate. I stood there for a few moments gathering my thoughts because this was mind-blowing. Then I took another deep breath and wondered how to start but it turned out to be easy. "Will Jack live?" Yellow lights blinked three times and soon I was asking questions and it answered each question promptly. Yes or no. Red or yellow.

Now and then it blinked both red and yellow at the same time so then I had to ask if it did so because the answer was both 'yes' and 'no' and it clearly blinked yellow three times to indicate that was what it was doing.

We could communicate. We *were* communicating.

Slowly, carefully, making sure each question could produce a useable answer, I found out that Jack needed rest so the lights were keeping him asleep but when his body recovered enough for him to wake up, they'd let it happen naturally. After he awoke, the lights said, he'd still need to rest for a while because his injuries were substantial. Life-threatening if the saucer hadn't brought him to a place capable of fixing his broken body.

The only problem with communicating with the facility – or with the saucer, I wasn't sure which -- was that the process was slow and tedious. Eventually I needed a break. I returned to the saucer, took a shower and made a pot of coffee. I brought that coffee back to Jack's room and sat for a while to decide what to ask next. Then, with a sigh and a realization that this would be neither quick nor easy, I settled in for a long and informative chat with a very large mechanical flying machine and/or the facility where it lived.

We were on the planet Mars, I learned, which wasn't as big a surprise as it might have been because I'd thought all along that we hadn't flown long enough to have returned to Earth. The facility on Mars was a smaller version of the one on Earth "Is this facility the only other one besides the one on Earth?" Three red blinks said there were more such places.

I asked about each of the other planets and their moons and the asteroid belt and learned that small facilities such as the one we were in were scattered throughout the solar system in strategic locations in case of emergencies or just as stopping places for patrols.

I also learned that the colors knew how to mend Jack's body because they knew about humans. How had they gotten that knowledge? The answer to that question was so complicated that I decided it would have to wait for another time when the answer could begin to unravel the whole flying saucer phenomenon. I figured it was such an overwhelming subject that it would take years for a simple, introductory conversation.

For now, Jack was my concern. I wanted to know when he'd be well enough for us to return to Earth. The saucer didn't have a good answer. When his body was sufficiently recovered was the best I could get with no timeline given no matter how many different ways I asked.

Jack would get well on his own schedule and humans were so varied the saucer didn't know how long it would take. Only when he was sufficiently healed, the saucer said, should we leave the facility.

So, I waited for Jack to wake up. Without access to the outside, I had no way of knowing how long he slept. I'd already done what Mazie had taught me to do when a transmission to Thom was essential and I figured this was such a time. After all, he did expect us back in a reasonable time and that time had come and gone.

Mazie had instructed me to not say a word about the Atlas Project or what I was doing or where I was if contact was necessary because transmissions could be intercepted. So, I created a coded message. I said we'd be staying longer than planned and would have an interesting tale to tell when we got home. I could have been talking about a tropical island vacation but Thom would know the truth. He didn't reply but, as Mazie had told me would happen, a 'beep' said he'd received the message and was okay with my plan.

I settled in to wait for Jack to wake up. I was

reading a book with Callie on my lap when that happened. I was in the chair beside his bed and was somewhat disconcerted to glance up and find his eyes on me. Sleepy, puzzled, looking from me to the unfamiliar room and back as he tried to make sense of what he saw.

Then his eyes closed again, and he slept some more. I put my book aside and watched for the next time his eyes came open and rehearsed once again the entire speech I'd so carefully prepared. All the love stuff and my promise not to pester him because of it.

I'd be polite, of course, but I'd make sure he knew how things were between us. I had it all planned, complete with expressive pauses and when to strategically look away. Except when he did wake for a second time, I forgot everything and found myself bawling happy tears. Me, the self-contained college student turned Atlas Project person.

Since a classroom type lecture doesn't go over well accompanied by tears I gave up on my well-honed speech and simply leaned over and kissed him chastely on the cheek. "Welcome back."

He smiled. Then he closed those beautiful blue eyes and went back to sleep, and I sighed and picked up my book again and hoped the next time he woke I'd be better prepared.

When it happened, I wasn't prepared any better than the first time, but he was more aware of his surroundings and before I had a chance to speak or cry or kiss him, he asked what was going on. "How'd you get to the facility so fast?"

"You've been asleep for a very long time."

He let that sink in. "However long it took, I'm glad

to be home. Even the facility looks good and it's the ugliest place I know." He lay back, exhausted from the effort of speaking. "I feel weak as a kitten."

"We aren't at the facility."

He looked around slowly. "It looks like the facility." He examined his surroundings for a long time. "Sort of looks like it. And also looks kind of like a hospital. Not exactly, but close." His eyes closed momentarily, and I held my breath but he opened them again with renewed vigor from the mini-rest. He was coming around quickly, and I gave an inner sigh of relief as he asked, "So if we aren't at the facility, where are we?"

"We're on Mars."

The eyes that had just opened went as wide as possible. He smiled tentatively at my joke. Then he knew it wasn't a joke and those eyes narrowed as he stared at me. He said, "Mars," in a neutral voice and then followed that with a question. "As in the planet Mars?"

I nodded and he was quiet for a long time, looking around and figuring out for himself what must have happened. It was in his examination of the room and the way he felt the sheet and blankets over him. But the final knowledge came as the lights emerged from the wall and danced around him. Entered him. Continued whatever they were doing to heal him.

It didn't hurt, I could see that, but he felt their presence in his body. When they faded back into the wall, he simply looked a question at me. I nodded slightly and his return look said it all. He knew, in a general way, what had happened. Now he wanted the details.

I got him caught up on everything that had happened. He remembered taking ore samples. He remembered the asteroid splitting in two and being somersaulted into space but nothing after that so the explanation was long. Every time I tried to skip something because he was growing weary, he'd stop me and insist I go over every tiny detail until he knew as much as I did.

Callie decided to keep him company. After all, he was her human. She jumped onto his bed and curled on his pillow. His smile said she was probably doing as much good as whatever the lights were doing, at least at this final stage of recovery. He needed rest and Callie made sure he got it. As his eyes closed at the end of the long rendition of the events of the past few days, I tiptoed to the second bed, crawled in, missing Callie on my pillow though I was glad she was with Jack. Then I slept.

When I awoke Jack was already awake and hungry. I decided that was a good sign and wondered if the lights had provided nourishment along with medication and had stopped because he was able to return to a normal diet. But Jack needed food and so did Callie, so instead of having a long-drawn-out conversation with the lights to find out what should be done, I high-tailed it to the saucer and made a simple meal that I brought back to Jack's room. He ate like he was starved. I took that as a good sign.

From that point on he recovered incredibly fast. At first, he tired easily, but improvements that I'd expected to take days or weeks took hours. The lights must have done some remarkable, ultra-advanced repair work on his body for him to get his strength back so quickly. I couldn't tell time in that place with no windows but in what I guessed were a few days he was restored to his previous health and ready to leave the hospital room and return to the saucer. And to his job in the Atlas Project.

CHAPTER EIGHTEEN

JACK INFORMED ME in his very Jack-like, brusque manner that he was both physically competent and ready to get back to work.

Okay, I thought. Good for you and that means you are also ready to hear the speech I'd been perfecting ever since I realized I was in love. The speech I'd failed to give so far. But it had to be said, I couldn't put it off forever, and I wasn't a coward. So I told myself I could do this and forced myself to look straight at him. "Jack," I started. "I have something to say."

He leaned back in his comfortable chair in the comfortable but small kitchen where we'd just had a meal which we both enjoyed more than eating in his hospital room. "What's up?"

I told myself I'd feel better for getting it over with even though at the moment I felt like yesterday's trash. I folded my hands demurely in my lap and spoke. "I'm in love with you." I went quiet to give him time to digest my words. Then I took a deep breath and prepared to continue. I knew what to say next. I'd memorized the whole speech.

I didn't get another word out because before I could say anything he was out of his chair and leaning over me, pulling me out of my chair, and hugging me. Then he was kissing me. No matter how I tried to mumble the first words of my speech I couldn't say anything.

I finally gave up and simply let the kiss happen, though in some remote part of my brain that was still functional I wondered how I'd feel when it ended because just where was this kiss going anyway? There were a thousand possibilities and his behavior until that moment wasn't promising if a long-term relationship was the goal. So I wondered about the future even as I kissed him back as hard as I knew how.

When he finally let up, he stared at me and said, "It's about time. I was beginning to think you had the emotions of a board."

"A board!" Of all the possibilities that had passed through the tiny fraction of my mind that was still functional during that kiss, this was the least likely. "Me? A board? Never!" How could he say such a thing! "And if that's what you thought, why'd you just kiss me?" The speech I'd practiced so hard was gone forever. "After ignoring me for weeks and weeks."

"It shouldn't be a surprise. I told you before you joined the patrol that I wanted you in my life. I said I'd be all over you."

"You said that but you never *did* anything. Not much, anyway. No real follow through. Until now."

"Yes, I did follow through. I did everything I could think of. I drove Thom crazy until he agreed to make us partners."

"But then you kept your distance. You were as remote as is possible in a spaceship. I thought you'd changed your mind."

"Of course, I kept my distance. You were a student until I came along. You were at college, not out in the world. You'd be there now learning who-knows-what if that avalanche hadn't buried your car. I was allowing for that difference. I was being considerate. I wasn't pushing you into something you might not be ready for. Because you were a student getting ready for life instead of actually living that life."

"I'm an adult and have been for some time and I've known what I wanted for just about forever and I knew I wanted you soon after meeting you."

"Maybe, but it still would have been wrong for me to come on strong, though goodness knows it took all my self-control not to, a fact that I believe I mentioned. So I figured you knew what I was doing. How considerate I was being." He raked his fingers through his hair. "Besides, I'm your boss. It's wrong for someone in authority to take advantage of a subordinate."

"I'm not a subordinate and you're not my boss. I'm your partner."

"Junior partner, still in training, so it would have been wrong. Until today when you said you love me. That made it right. That changed things. As long as you weren't under duress when you said it."

"I wasn't."

His eyes shone. His whole being shone and that warmed me in a way I'd not thought possible as he added, "I'd about given up on getting some kind of signal from you."

I took a deep breath. Blew it out slowly. Went deep inside of me the better to experience the warm feeling that was spreading throughout my body now that I kind of knew where this was going even as I wondered why it had taken us so long to get to this place. And I asked the most important question of all. "Are you in love with me?"

"Of course, I am. I told you so before and I'm saying it again now."

"You never used the word 'love.' You said you wanted me in your life. That's different."

He scowled. "Different words. Same meaning. I love you." We stared at each other. "I hope you understand that because I don't know any other way to say it."

"You love me. You truly love me. And I love you."

It was amazing. Absolutely amazing.

We went silent. Stared at each other. Didn't know what to say or what to do until a grin – maybe not a grin, maybe a smile – spread across his face. "Are we a couple of idiots or what?"

"We must be." I found myself smiling along with him. I smiled so hard I thought my face would break.

"Got lots to make up for."

He moved close and that was the end of any and all conversation for a long, long time.

Much later Jack looked around the room and whispered in my ear which was easy because we were very, very close. "We have recently learned that the saucer hears everything we say. Do you think it sees everything we do, too?"

"Probably." I looked where he was looking but didn't see any eyes staring our way. "I'm sure it's watching us right now."

"And wondering what those weird humans are

doing." With which he nuzzled my ear again.

"Is there any place private on this saucer?"

"I doubt it but I'm not going to worry about some machine seeing me with the woman I love." He blew in my ear. "Maybe it'll learn something. Maybe it'll start a file on human love."

The rest of that day – as best days could be counted where there was no way to tell time – was spent getting to know each other on a deeper level than I'd thought possible. We even forgot Callie existed until she reminded us loudly that she was still there and needed cuddles and food.

The next day we got around to discussing the future and among the topics under discussion was the fact that we should head home. "Thom is probably crazy from wondering why we're still gone and what we'll have to say when we return."

"Yes, we should go home."

But we didn't move. We simply sat because everything that had happened had left us weak as spaghetti. Even learning we were mutually in love, instead of invigorating us, had had the odd effect of making us both so relaxed a feather could have knocked us over.

We just kept grinning and grinning. Then we grinned all over again. I felt like I was living in a dream and the fact that we were on another planet somehow multiplied the feeling a hundred-fold.

And so we sat, Jack with his feet on a table and me spread out in a comfortable chair until he said, "We should make plans. Do something."

"Yes, we should. What kind of plan?" I moved slightly in my chair because there were probably things we should discuss though I had no idea what they might be and didn't really care all that much. The chair was comfortable, the day was lovely, and Jack was close by. What more could I want?

After a good two minutes during which we neither said nor did anything, Jack continued. "I've known all along I want you in my life. As far as I'm concerned, that means we get married but if you aren't a fan of marriage then some other arrangement can be worked out."

"I'm a believer in marriage."

"Good. Then I'm asking you right here and now to marry me."

"And I'm answering 'yes' right here and now."

Did we jump up and down and celebrate? Nope. We continued to just sit because it was absolutely overwhelming that the man I loved was in love with me, we were both members of the Atlas Project, and we'd just agreed to get married.

I decided in some remote corner of my mind that the icing on the cake was that we were on Mars and somehow that made all those other things even more special. And yet all we did was smile at one another and take another sip of coffee until Jack said we should do something. Celebrate in some way.

Yes, we probably should. Somehow.

A cunning look came across his face. "We're on Mars, I feel back to good health, and we aren't expected back at any particular time." Our lethargy disappeared instantly, both mine and Jack's. Our gazes met and I waited for him to tell me what he had in mind. "We should do something to celebrate both the fact that we are on Mars and that we are a team in every way possible, professional and personal." His expression grew brighter. Like a kid with a candy cane. "Something special."

"Such as?"

"We should do a little exploring."

"Thom would approve because that's what the Atlas Project does."

"And it'll be awesome. And fun."

We were members of the Atlas Project and exploring strange planets was what we did. What any member of the Patrol would do. Plus, it would be amazing to tell our grandchildren some day that we went for a walk on Mars to celebrate getting engaged.

But what had happened on the asteroid had made me cautious. Jack tried to assuage my fears. "Mars isn't an asteroid that can break apart at any moment. It's a planet. It's solid and should be safe. We can take a walk."

"Are you sure? Have you ever been here before?"

"On Mars? No. I've been other places in the solar system but never on Mars."

"There might be dangers."

We asked the saucer, reasoning it should know about Mars since it had a facility there. Since I'd been the one who spoke with it before I was the one who asked questions while Jack watched to see how this unusual form of communication worked. "Is Mars solid?" Yes, I was informed.

"Can we go outside on Mars safely?" That answer was ambiguous. Both red and yellow, which meant I'd better ask more questions.

"Is Mars safe if we wear space suits?" Still ambiguous. Both red and yellow.

Frustrated, I asked, "Is there a way to be safe on Mars?" Yellow, which meant there was a safe way so we could take that walk if I could find out how to be safe by asking only questions that could be answered with 'yes' or 'no.'

It took a long time and a lot of questions to discover the saucer could make space suits that would be a thousand times better, safer, and greatly superior to the one that had almost killed Jack. It took an equal number of questions to learn how to go about getting such a suit. The answer, when I finally got it, was simple. The saucer would make the suits and they'd be tailored for each of us.

I told the saucer to create space suits. Immediately a glow appeared a few feet in front of each of us, small at first, but growing until they were slightly larger than our bodies. We glanced at each other for reassurance and then stepped into the glow. As soon as I was inside, the glow changed. Morphed. Became a lightweight, subtly glowing golden suit that fit like a glove and was about an inch thick with a clear faceplate and a backpack the size of one of my mother's purses.

I told the saucer I had more questions that needed answers. Our suits disappeared. "Will we be able to breathe?" We wondered because that tiny oxygen backpack seemed too small but it turned out that the answer was a definite 'yes' because oxygen was created and replenished from local resources instead of being hauled on our backs. The backpack didn't carry oxygen. Instead, it made it.

The saucer had been right about everything so far so we decided to trust it for oxygen. Though I could see that Jack had no qualms about our new suits, I decided

I'd go outside cautiously, taking baby steps so I could duck back immediately if I found myself short of breath.

I asked about a hundred more questions to learn what to do if something went wrong. Again, a precaution after what happened on the asteroid. Turned out our new space suits were equipped with built-in monitors that would alert the saucer if anything went wrong at which time it would automatically reel us in like a couple of fish unless we had wandered so far that that feature wouldn't work. It depended on the tractor beam and that had a limited reach.

If we were beyond that reach, though, we learned that we could call the saucer for help. It would hear us from anywhere on the planet or beyond.

Satisfied that we'd be reasonably safe we headed for the bridge. Jack piloted us out of the landing strip through what turned out to be the huge cave that held the Mars facility and onto a flat, red sand dune.

I made sure the saucer knew we were going outside so it would be listening for any communications. Jack set the control panel to automatic with specific instructions to wait for further instructions. Then I called once more for suits, we stepped into them, held hands because the being in love thing was still new and we wanted to experience it to the max, and headed for the airlock. Almost as an afterthought, though I'd already learned that nothing was an afterthought in the Atlas Project, Jack grabbed a couple of ropes with carabiners that we wrapped around our waists.

Soon we stood on the red sand of Mars. We were in an area of rough terrain that was strange and strangely beautiful. We turned around several times before he asked, "Which way?"

I looked around. "Every direction is the same."

So, we went straight ahead because that was as good a way as any. And we went for a walk on Mars.

CHAPTER NINETEEN

THE NEW AND improved space suits fit like gloves and allowed for reasonably easy movement. With the reduced gravity of Mars, we were able to cover a lot of ground in a short time. I looked back and was surprised how far we'd come. "Too far to be hauled back if there's trouble."

Jack checked the distance we'd traveled and nodded then looked ahead. "The terrain ahead is getting rough. It'll be interesting."

There were buttes ahead that would block our view of the saucer once we reached them, and boulders were strewn about the landscape as if tossed by a giant. One formation, though, caught our attention. It was somehow different. "Is that a canyon?"

We sped up, eager to see what lay ahead. Turned out it wasn't a canyon. Rather it was an opening in the ground perhaps a hundred feet deep and we could see where the opening turned into long, narrow caves on either side of the hole. "It's a lava tube. It could go for miles." What we'd mistaken for a canyon was where the top of the lava tube had caved in, leaving a jagged hole in the landscape.

We tried to see where the lava tube went. It

appeared to go straight in either direction. When we looked along the tube toward its beginning, we saw what must at one time have been a volcano. "The volcano erupted, and the lava ran down here and made a long, narrow cave."

"I'd love to see the volcano but it's pretty far away."

"This is Mars. One third gravity. We can walk just about forever in hardly any time at all." We judged that it was several miles away but, as Jack said, on Mars it should be an easy stroll. So, we set off.

Neither of us was concerned when those boulders and buttes cut off our view of the saucer. If we got lost, we could call the saucer and ask for directions. Of course, I'd have to ask in a way that could be answered by 'yes' or 'no' but I was growing proficient at that odd means of communication.

We reached the volcano. It had been dead for so many millions of years that it was now a gently sloped hill. We reached the top and found a large rock to stand on to better survey the planet in every direction. We turned around several times to see everything. It was awesome with the black sky above and the rust red landscape spreading below. We were glad we'd come.

"There's an aurora." Jack pointed to waving lights in the sky. "Not as spectacular as on Earth but lovely."

"And something else," I called his attention to a different direction and pointing. "What's that?"

It took a few moments to figure out what we were looking at. "Is that dust?" The horizon blurred, almost like a cloud but Mars lacked water.

"Sandstorm," Jack said with a slight touch of concern.

We watched for a minute or so. "It's coming this way."

"Storms on Mars can be bad. Very bad."

Rovers on Mars had been trapped by sandstorms. I'd followed their adventures with interest. They'd been forced into sleep mode so couldn't send pictures to truly show what the storms were like. How much visibility there was. How dangerous they were.

"We should get back." Jack jumped from our rock. "Now." I followed. Soon we were running, hopping and jumping towards the saucer. We made amazing progress, almost flying across the red ground with that lava tube hole as our goal since we couldn't see the saucer.

We were fast but the storm was faster. We hadn't gone very far when we were almost blown off our feet and encased in a cloud of sand. We stopped long enough to adjust and to hook our suits together with one of the ropes he'd brought. Otherwise, we could have gotten separated.

We resumed moving but slower, more carefully. Jack spoke through our helmet comms. "Do you know where we are? I can't see a thing." The sand whipped around cruelly and wrapped us in a rust-colored blanket.

"I don't have a clue, nor do I know which direction is right."

"Call the saucer," Jack said grimly. "We can't chance going in the wrong direction."

We stopped. Jack came close enough to see me through our face plates. He tried to be nonchalant but he didn't fool me. He was worried.

It was easy to establish communication with the

saucer but I could only ask questions that could be answered with 'yes' or 'no' and that slowed everything down to a snail's pace as the storm raged.

Yes, the saucer had our coordinates. A yellow light in my helmet said so. Yes, it could send up a bright light – and it did – but we couldn't see anything because the blowing sand was too dense or else because the buttes and boulders blocked our view. The cardinal directions were no help because we were on Mars. No magnetic poles so no working compass.

Fear crawled into my stomach and wrapped around my gut as I tried to think what questions would get us back to the saucer. But how do you get directions when all reference points are obscured by sand, a compass is useless, and there's no beacon to home in on?

Except there was a way. Perhaps. "I can ask the saucer if we're going in the right direction. It'll answer 'yes' or 'no' and we'll adjust our direction accordingly.

We walked a bit. Then we stopped and I asked the saucer if it was the right direction. It replied that 'yes' we were headed towards it. "It's like the kids' game. Yellow when going the right way and red if we're wrong."

And so we walked. A half dozen steps followed by a yellow or red light indicating whether we were on the right path or the wrong one, after which we'd either keep walking or adjust our direction.

Our journey was agonizingly slow but we'd end up in the right place and that was all that mattered. We actually walked into a boulder once because we didn't see it and so plowed right into it. The sandstorm was that thick. The good thing was that boulder meant we were once more in the area where the lava tube had caved in. The area of buttes and boulders. We were more than half-way home.

We kept walking. "Nothing to it," Jack said as we lengthened our strides because the sandstorm was getting worse and the saucer would be warm and comfortable and wouldn't have a grain of sand in it.

One step, then another, with each step as long as possible because this was Mars, and we could go three times as fast and as far as on Earth. Encouraged, I took a huge step. A leap.

And I leaped into thin air.

CHAPTER TWENTY

I FELL, PLUNGING down, down, down into a hole. A cave. The lava tube I'd forgotten about in my eagerness to reach the saucer.

We were roped together. I pulled Jack with me. We tumbled, fell, slid and rolled seemingly forever. I panicked. What if we tore our suits? What would happen? But the saucer-made suits were impervious to the jagged edges we hit. Our bodies, on the other hand, were fragile and when we finally hit bottom we were stunned and in pain.

Mars' lesser gravity was the only reason we were still alive. The tumble down the rough side of the hole must have been at least a hundred feet. On Earth we'd not have survived. The only good thing was that the sandstorm was nonexistent so deep down and we could see our surroundings.

"Elena! Elana! Are you okay?"

I rolled over towards Jack's voice. We were still roped together, and he lay not far away. I had to untangle the rope before I could see him. "I think I'm good. What about you?"

A moment's silence as he moved one body part

and then another. "I seem to be in one piece though I'm going to have bruises everywhere and I'll hurt for a long time."

I moved experimentally. Then I cautiously sat up. "Me too. Except for my face. The helmet protected me." I fought tears. "I did this Jack. I was in a hurry. I took a wrong step."

"Not your fault. Things happen and neither of us could see in the storm." His words were balm but didn't negate my responsibility for what had happened. Would we survive? Had I gotten us both killed?

We crawled towards each other and hugged awkwardly through the suits. Then Jack spoke in a voice so normal I knew it was an act. "Let's see what things look like so we can figure how to get out of here."

"We're pretty far down."

"Getting up will be like climbing a mountain but people climb them all the time. Mars gravity should make it three times easier than with any mountain on Earth."

Moving hurt. Bad. The simplest movement was agonizing but necessary as we uncoupled from each other. Jack looped the rope around his waist once more, each movement a sympathy of pain.

Even as we hated to move, we realized how fortunate we were that neither of us had broken bones. Were the suits the reason? Had their superior design protected us from serious injuries?

We reached the wall we'd have to climb. Jack pulled a small but powerful flashlight from the bag of tools that hung from his waist and examined it closely. Then he snapped it off to save the battery as we internalized what we'd seen.

"It's as smooth as glass down this far. Only the top is rough." I ran a hand over the rock wall and even through the suit it felt like a polished mirror.

"No handholds. No ledges. Nothing but smooth rock until too far up for us to reach." Far enough to know there was no way we'd be able to climb our way out of the lava tube cave.

"We need another idea." Jack was once again determinedly casual but I wasn't fooled.

I looked into the darkness on either side of us. The tube that started at the dead volcano and came to where we fell through a cave-in and then continued on. "Can we walk out?"

"Let's find out."

We forced our bodies to move through pain. But we didn't walk far because when the roof of the lava tube caved in debris closed off the tube where it came from the volcano. "It was the wrong direction anyway," I said as cheerfully as possible, trying to emulate Jack's positive attitude.

We turned and headed the other way. At least that part of the lava tube pointed to the general direction of the saucer. But that also proved to be a dead end. Not because debris blocked the way but because it suddenly, abruptly, dropped another hundred or so feet and we weren't about to go any farther down in the Martian landscape than we already had gone.

We returned to where we landed. "We can't walk out," Jack said, despair creeping around the edges of his voice. "And even if we can climb out, we still have to get to the saucer and we're both hurting so bad I'm not sure we can make walk that far."

"Too bad the saucer can't come to us."

We looked at each other as the realization came to us that perhaps the saucer could do exactly that. "Saucers patrol autonomously. No pilots. They've been doing so for centuries. Possibly millions of years."

"But Thom deactivated the program that controlled that function."

Jack looked at me. It was hard to make out his features in the dark cave and through the faceplate, but hope was plain to see. The man was a living, breathing believer in happy endings. "Talk to the saucer, Elena. Find out if it can come to us."

"We'll still have to climb out ourselves. It's too deep for the tractor beam to reach us and the saucer won't fit in the hole."

"It'll be better than what we're doing now, which is nothing. It'll at least be closer. We'll figure something out." He refused to give up and his stubbornness was contagious. "It's what we do." He grinned a lopsided grin, adding, "We're the Atlas Project. We can't let a little thing like a hundred-foot glass-like cliff slow us down."

I spoke to the saucer. Yes, it could come to us if I ordered it to. So of course, I gave the order and soon it was hovering over the cave opening, hanging above us unaffected by the sandstorm. I told it to use the tractor beam and bring us out of the cave.

As expected, it didn't work. We could see the beam light up the upper part of the cave but it didn't reach the bottom. "So close," Jack said in frustration.

We slumped on the ground against a large rock and stared at the beam that was so tantalizingly close but not close enough. Jack said morosely, "A halfway decent pitcher could throw a baseball and hit the light." He gave a huge sigh and stared at the tractor beam.

"Did you play baseball when you were a kid?"

"Some."

"Were you a pitcher?"

"No. I was an outfielder."

"Outfielders throw balls a fair distance. From the outfield to home plate."

He looked up thoughtfully and considered the distance to the tractor beam. "I might be able to toss a ball that high. But what good would it do?" It was a question, not a comment. He hoped I had a way to get us out of there. "Even if the tractor beam caught the ball we'd still be stuck down here. And we don't have a ball."

"What if you threw a rock with the rope wrapped around it so it would connect us to the tractor beam? But it would be heavier than a baseball. Do you think you could do that?"

His face lit up. "It's a long shot. But I can try. Better than doing nothing." He moved and doubled over with pain. "Must be the right sized rock and remember that I'm not major league material."

The cave was littered with rocks of all sizes but finding the right one was difficult. We looked for a long time, stooping to see better and fighting pain with every step but eventually Jack held a rock in his hand and hefted it. "It's decent. The best we're likely to find." He looked at me. "We wrap the rock with rope and tie it tight like you said. But before we do that, we tie the second rope to both of us so when the tractor beam catches the rock it'll haul both of us up along with the rope."

"Think it'll work? The two of us together?"

"We're not separating. We're not going up one at a time. No way."

"It'll be extremely painful and we're already hurting bad."

"Can't help that."

"It's the only way?"

"If we want to go home."

"I'll tell the saucer what to do. I'll tell it to be gentle."

We worked slowly because pain wouldn't allow for anything else. When the rock was as secure as we could make it, we tied ourselves together with the second rope, the one around my waist, and then we clipped both ropes to Jack's waist and then to mine until we were wrapped together as thoroughly as a Christmas package.

I ordered the saucer to catch the rock Jack would throw into the tractor beam. He'd left his throwing arm free. He swung the rock around and around like David swung his sling when he fought Goliath. When the rock was whizzing around as fast as possible, he aimed it at the tractor beam and let go.

We held our breath. The rock arced upwards until it reached the bottom edge of the beam exactly as it reached the end of the rope. It stopped. Hung there a second as the saucer tried to capture it. And dropped back to the floor of the cave.

"You did it. You threw it almost high enough. You can throw it high enough."

"The rope isn't long enough."

"We have a second rope."

"It's what holds us together."

"We have no choice."

Jack gave me a long look before he said, "We use the second rope to get the rock into the tractor beam and we'll both be pulled up because we'll hold onto each other so hard there won't be any possibility of either of us falling."

"What if one of us falls anyway?"

"That won't happen. It can't happen."

"Or it will happen and will be fatal because we are already fragile after the original fall into the cave."

"We'll make it because we'll be so tight together a piece of paper won't fit between us." I could see his lips pressed together behind his face plate. "There's no possibility of us not making it and we'll both be okay. We'll be drinking coffee and eating donuts in no time."

I looked up at the saucer. So close and yet so far away. I wanted to order it to come into the cave but the opening was too small and breaking through could send rocks hurtling down on us. We couldn't risk it.

We unwrapped the rope that held us together and clipped it to the end of the first rope. Jack started to clip the other end of the rope to my space suit but I stopped him. "You're stronger than me. If I'm the one clipped to the rope, I'll have to both keep hold of the rope and of you. But if you're the one clipped to the rope, you're strong enough to do it and believe me I'll hold onto you. But the important thing is, you're larger than me. Stronger. There's more chance of success that way."

He reluctantly moved the clip to his space suit. "Hang on to me and I'll hang on to you." He didn't want it to be that way but it was the best way. The only way. "Don't let go no matter what happens."

I climbed onto Jack's back and wrapped both my

arms and legs around his body and tucked my head into his shoulder as best I could considering the bulk of the space suit and helmet. It was only possible because of the lighter, slimmer suits the saucer had made.

I spoke to the saucer. "Jack's throwing the rock now. Grab it and slowly, gently, pull us up."

Jack repeated his first throw. The sling whizzed around and around until he released it and it fairly flew higher and higher until it reached the tractor beam. As the first time, it hung in the air for a moment, and we held our breath. I thought it was higher into the beam than before. But was it high enough?

We waited for the rock to fall back to the ground. Instead, it hung in the air far longer than would happen naturally. Then it hung there longer. And still longer. And slowly, gently, we felt the tug on the rope clipped to Jack's suit that said the rock was far enough inside the tractor beam to be secure and the saucer was starting to pull us up.

We went up slowly. As gently as possible. But we also rotated. We swung back and forth. We twisted. We moved so many ways as we went upwards that I couldn't keep a grip on Jack. I felt myself coming loose. Jack felt it too. "Hold on, Elena. Hold hard."

He grabbed my arms with his. He tried to grab my legs with his and hold tight. It worked until we started spinning crazily. I felt the two of us slowly separating.

"Nooooo!" Jack screamed as he grabbed tighter. Held me harder. But nothing could stop the slow separation because our suits, even though they were less bulky than the first suits we'd had, were thick enough to prevent either of us from gripping truly tight.

Jack tore at his space suit. He screamed through his

helmet. He'd never before spoken to the saucer because that had been my job but he did it then. "Remove the gloves from my suit!" It was an order. "Let my hands be free."

As if by magic, the gloves on his suit disappeared and Jack grabbed me with all the strength he had. It worked. The separation of our bodies stopped. I scrunched closer to him, and he held me tight.

But Mars was cold. Way below zero. How long could his unprotected hands remain in that cold without them freezing? How close were we to the tractor beam? When we reached it would it be warm enough to keep his hands from freezing? Or was the temperature in the beam the same as the surrounding atmosphere?

But no matter what happened to his hands, we had to go slowly. We couldn't risk coming apart. We reached the lower edge of the beam, the part with filtered light that wasn't strong enough to hold anything. The area the first throw had reached. "Faster," I yelled to the saucer, and we moved upwards quicker.

Then we were in the true light of the beam. It was brilliant. But was it warm or cold? I didn't know, I was fully suited. "Faster," I yelled again, and we found ourselves shooting upwards. We'd be in the saucer in moments. Would those seconds be enough to save Jack's hands? At least it didn't matter how hard we held onto each other. We were in the tractor beam and that held us both securely.

We tumbled into an open airlock. The door closed. Air rushed in. We removed our helmets and then our suits. And Jack examined his hands.

"They're good," he said grinning.

"Not frozen?"

"The beam was as warm as a sunny day in Florida. Not even any frostbite."

I fell against him in relief as he said simply, "Let's get that coffee and donuts."

He was being a big, brave macho male. "Is that all you can say after we just about died?"

He shrugged. "Get used to it, Elena. We're the Atlas Project. We patrol the solar system. It's what we do." But he couldn't keep a grin from spreading until his face glowed from it and we headed into the saucer kitchen and soon were enjoying ourselves.

"We should head for the infirmary and see what parts of us need repair."

"In a bit. Right now, I just want to enjoy being alive."

When the coffee and donuts were gone and we'd had enough time to decompress, we headed for the infirmary and learned that nothing was broken, and the bruises would heal on their own so all we needed was pain relievers and the saucer had plenty of those.

We spent the remainder of that Martian day filling out patrol logs and trying to put into words what had happened. If it was day as we sat at the desks that appeared like magic when I said we needed them.

We didn't know what time it was any more than we'd known day from night in the enclosed Martian facility. The sandstorm was still hiding the sun and our only reference was our stomachs and we'd just had a snack so hunger wasn't any help.

We finally decided it might be evening so we had a light dinner and then we sat in comfortable chairs and shoved the reports aside and talked for hours because there was no way either of us would be able to sleep. Not after what we'd just gone through.

CHAPTER TWENTY-ONE

OUR RETURN TO Earth was slow. Very slow considering the speeds saucers are capable of. We each thought the other would want to push the saucer now that we had some kind of relationship with it – communication being a kind of relationship -- but that turned out to be wrong. Neither of us wanted to push our craft.

We not only didn't push the saucer, we were super cautious. Extra vigilant. We avoided looking at each other for a while because we both felt foolish. We thought the other would say there was no reason to be careful. Except there was a reason and we eventually learned we both felt the same way. We'd had enough experience with things going wrong that we'd have taken a year to return if such was indicated.

As it was, it took the same amount of time to return from Mars as it had taken to reach it on our way to the asteroid belt. But the return trip felt different. Anticlimactic. For whatever the reason, getting home took weeks, during which time we watched the stars, slept, read, and talked.

"I want your opinion about something," Jack said

one day after shoving aside the computer where we'd been recording the endless reports that went with every patrol. You'd think that since we weren't the government, we wouldn't have to do so much, but Thom insisted we document everything that happened on a patrol. Every. Single. Thing. I wondered if any patrol before this one had ever had so much to document. Probably not.

Jack's comment had been intentional, and I knew it. He was making sure I was paying attention because what was to come was important. I knew because by then I knew him well. So I shoved aside my own computer and listened as he spoke. "Who knows what the future will hold?" He looked at me hard. "I want to experience married life before something bad happens."

"Too late. Bad has already happened."

"Something worse."

"Nothing bad will happen ever again because we are being the most careful people in the solar system. Look how slowly we're going home."

"Slow doesn't necessarily mean safe. Not in this business."

He was right. Things could still go wrong. But they wouldn't. Somehow, I knew that but I agreed with him about getting married as soon as possible. "If I'm honest I admit I don't want to wait any longer either. A future as a married woman appeals to me." I didn't repeat what he'd just pointed out, that our wonderful future could be dangerous but he knew what was behind my carefully chosen words.

So, we talked and planned and one day in the middle of an Antarctic blizzard that was identical to the sandstorm on Mars except it was white snow instead of reddish sand, the saucer dropped into the ocean and moments later came up and glided to a stop on the facility landing strip. We were home.

Thom didn't know we were coming so there was no one to greet us. We strolled down the ramp and didn't know where to go. What to do. "The kitchen. That's where all the action is."

"Thom is probably there." After all, it was lunch time if anyone was paying attention to the time. Atlas Project members in the facility did look at clocks once in a while to keep in sync with the outside world. The kitchen was a good place to look for our boss.

He was there and almost choked on his lunch when he saw us. He rose, mouth full of food, and came running. "You're back. About time. What amazing things are you going to tell me?" He pulled us both to the table and shoved his lunch aside as he sat us down, eyes blazing. "It had better be important because I've been going crazy since getting your message and I don't want all those sleepless nights to have been wasted."

So, we told him the saucers can communicate. His eyes grew large, and he just stared at us for a long time. "Tell me everything. Absolutely everything. Don't leave out a single second of how you discovered such an amazing thing and I'll bet it'll be a story to tell the next generation. And the generation after that."

We told him everything and only left out those things that were personal. No need for him to know about us, not yet. But we spoke of the asteroid and the ore that could be mined there. We told him about the asteroid breaking in half and what happened after that. About our new space suits. And how tractor beams can be used to rescue Patrol members in trouble. Most of all, we explained how we communicated with the saucer.

By the time our story wound down, there were several members of the Patrol sitting around listening intently, including Mazie and Brock. We could see eagerness in everyone's eyes. They wanted to see for themselves everything we were explaining and experience it first-hand. They could hardly wait.

When we were done talking, Thom and everyone else headed for the saucer hanger to try out our new communication method while Jack and I headed for our rooms. Actually, our one room because we were beyond separating after our trip so we informed Callie that she and Jack would be visiting me for a while and we three – two people and a kitten – went to my room where we all three dropped onto my bed and slept as deeply as if we'd never slept before.

The next day Thom was practically flying. He was that excited. "I've been talking with the saucer all night."

"Talking? We could only get 'yes' and 'no' answers."

He shook his head impatiently. "That's how we talked. I asked questions and it answered. But it was a real conversation. Sort of a conversation, anyway. I learned a lot and we're just getting started."

"It's a very slow way to communicate. We learned that on patrol."

"Slow now, I agree. But things will be different when we can truly communicate. When the saucer speaks."

"With words?" We looked warily at each other.

English was about as far from colors as we could imagine. "In English?"

"Yes, English."

"How'd you work that miracle?"

"I haven't yet. It'll be a while. Not long, though. Just long enough for me to design a translator device and for the saucers to manufacture one. Then a lot of them. One for each saucer. Think what it'll mean. You can talk with the saucers while on patrol. You and the saucers can work together as a team. It'll be a whole new way of patrolling the solar system."

"They can make a translator device?"

"They can indeed, and we know their abilities because of you, Elena. When you communicated with the saucer you also learned it could make space suits. And it did. Think how complicated space suits are. How many things they must do, what all they must monitor, and they do all those things simultaneously. If the saucer can make superior space suits, then making a device to translate colors into English will be child's play."

"Can they design a translator device?"

His face dimmed a bit. "I'll have to do that. They say they don't know how."

"Can you do it?"

"Of course, I can. It'll take a while, of course. It'll be a whole new kind of science. Colors aren't normally used for communication except with signal flags. But it's eminently doable and I intend to do it as soon as possible. I plan to have a nice, long conversation with a saucer in English and I'll do before you two slowpokes get around to figuring out that you're meant for each other."

Jack and I both flushed, then Jack said, "We've already figured that out."

"What? You have?" He stopped in his headlong rush towards scientific discovery to nod briefly. "About time. I was about to give up on you. So was everyone else. We had a betting pool going and were about to give up on you two ever getting together. We'd decided to cash it in for leather jackets for everyone. With Atlas Project on the back."

"No need now. We're engaged. Did you win the pool?"

"No. I thought you'd take longer. I think Brock came close, though. He said being on patrol would do it and evidently, he was right." He shook his head and forgot all about Jack and me and our life and future as he returned to his one true love. Flying saucers.

Soon he was on his way to his workshop by the landing strip where we were sure he was doing all kinds of things we couldn't comprehend so flying saucers and people could have a conversation.

Over the next few days and weeks, as patrols returned to the facility, they stayed because Thom decided no patrols should be planned until the communication device was operational. No matter how long we waited, he said, the time involved would be miniscule compared to how long the saucers had been going on unmanned patrols before he came along and how long we'd be on patrol with them as partners.

So, we members of the Atlas Project played cards. And read books. And watched movies. And did exercises and ran foot races through the endless corridors and managed a game of baseball in the viewing room that ended when a foul ball broke a window.

We played with Callie and the mother cat and the rest of the kittens. Jack and I planned our future during long, leisurely hours of watching the cold Antarctic weather from the warmth of the viewing room once the broken window had been replaced.

It was exactly what we needed. Time to unwind and we knew we'd finally succeeded in doing just that when we became bored and wished Thom would hurry so we could go on patrol once more. The rest of the Patrol had felt that way for a long time and everyone was growing restless. We wanted action. We felt rudderless.

But it finally happened. One day Thom corralled everyone in the kitchen – the default meeting place – and informed us that we could all head to the saucer hanger and have a conversation with a bunch of machines. A bunch of flying saucers. In English.

What happened next was both disappointing and more amazing than I'd have believed possible. Disappointing because the saucers were no different than before we could converse with them. They were still flying saucers. Machines. Inanimate objects. Amazing because they talked with us and their side of the conversations actually made sense.

Thom started off. "Saucer." Nothing obvious happened. No sudden springing to attention by the saucers. No lights flickering. No noises emanating from any of them. Then he said, "What time is it by the clocks in the facility?"

A rusty-sounding voice said, "One-thirty PM."

Someone behind me said, "Really Thom? Couldn't you come up with a more realistic voice for our friends?" Everyone else clapped and cheered.

Thom wasn't insulted. "Stop complaining and be glad they can talk." Followed by laughter. "An innovation that might save your life someday."

Everyone wanted a turn talking with the saucers. I was first because I'd discovered their communication abilities. Thom gestured for me to say something or ask a question. I thought for a while, then asked the one thing I'd most wondered about while in space. While waiting for Jack and the saucer to pluck me out of the lava tube cave. While wondering if the saucer was watching Jack and me. "Are you sentient?"

The place went silent. Everyone wanted to know though we all thought we knew the answer.

We were wrong. The saucer said, "No."

"Are you sure?"

"We are machines. Machines are not sentient."

"Do you understand the meaning of sentience?"

"I do."

I still didn't believe it so I asked another question. "Are you capable of considering existence beyond what's required for the completion of your missions?"

The answer was a simple, "No."

"But you speak coherently. You converse with us."

"We have no need to be sentient. We have no desire to be sentient." I thought there was expression in the answer. Perhaps distaste. As if sentience was too horrible a fate to contemplate and it felt sorry for us poor sentient beings but good manners prohibited it from saying so. "But we are very good machines. Very, very excellent ones."

Jack whispered because in spite of what the saucer had just said, none of us were sure what would happen if the saucers heard us talking about them. They might not be sentient but who knew how advanced they were in some other way we couldn't comprehend? Some way that was beyond anything we could even imagine. We didn't want to take any chances on making them unhappy. So, he whispered. "Sounds like they don't want to be sentient."

I whispered back. "Which might make them smarter than we realize. Or not as smart."

The rest of the Patrol took turns talking with the saucers. Some asked technical questions about missions and got extremely technical answers. Others wanted to know what it was like to be a flying saucer, which elicited no true response because the saucers couldn't describe what they were like any more than we could accurately describe being human. Some questions got an 'ambivalent question,' response followed by silence. What would once have been both yellow and red before they communicated with words.

Eventually there were no more questions so Patrol members straggled out of the hanger and ended up in the kitchen to discuss a future with flying saucers that would now be full partners even if they were machines. Very advanced machines.

I wondered how the saucers would look at our partnership. If they'd even consider us as actual partners. If so, did they consider us equal partners or were we lesser ones? The next time I was in one and we got into a conversation, I'd ask. I had no idea what the answer would be.

The patrol talked for hours in the kitchen. They made pots of coffee, and someone found some cookies to dip in it.

Jack and I contemplated the feet draped over tables and how some of the Patrol leaned so far back in their chairs that their balance was at stake. We decided they'd only stop discussing talking machines when they were too tired to stay awake and they'd probably get back to talking as soon as they arose the next day because being able to communicate with saucers was that big of a deal.

It was important. We both knew that. It would change all of our lives and the Patrol wanted to discuss the details. But we were weeks ahead of them in that department. We'd been communicating with a saucer for a while already. So, we eventually left them and retired to my apartment to discuss a future that was important and not just because it included saucers. Because it was our future.

CHAPTER TWENTY-TWO

THOM GAVE US time off. "You deserve it." His only reference to what had happened on my first official patrol.

We used the time to get married.

Jack's parents were overjoyed when they found out. They'd given up on their son ever settling down. "It's that secret job of his, whatever it is," his mother said as she hugged me and assured me that they were totally in favor of me and of our marriage. "He never had a chance to meet anyone until you came along. We consider ourselves fortunate that now he's going to have at least a close to normal life."

My parents said pretty much the same thing when we saw them after leaving Jack's parents' home. When the two sets of parents finally got together at the wedding, they just about fell into each other's arms with relief that their children were going to have a semi-normal life.

My brother Pete saw things a little differently. "So, they let you guys out of jail long enough to get married." He approved of Jack because Jack approved of classic cars. "Big of them, whoever they are." Then he surprised both of us by asking, "By the way, just out of curiosity, what are the requirements for going to work at this super-secret place?"

Jack eyed his future brother-in-law. "Why are you asking?"

Pete shrugged. "It sounds interesting." Then he shuddered. "Not my thing but it's clearly what my baby sister wants so I'll always wonder." Then he added, grinning, "It must be interesting. Top secret and all."

"It is," both Jack and I said together.

My father said slowly, "The fact that you both said the same thing at the same time means this secretive job is way more than any of us suspected when you first came around." His eyes narrowed but he refrained from asking more questions because he knew there was nothing we could say to either affirm or deny any of it.

He was right about one thing. Our lives would be different from most. Were already different. It was like living two lives, one in the normal world and one in the world of flying saucers, and those lives never met except for the one time – one day – when we got married in the back yard overlooking the field and the tiny woods where Jack had passed on Thom's invitation to join the Atlas Project. A short engagement because we were still on leave and would have to get back to work shortly so we wanted to get it done.

Thom came to the wedding. So did Mazie and Brock and most of the Atlas Project people. Of course, none of them could say where they were from, what they did for a living, or anything else most people talk about as a way of making conversation so there were some awkward moments until the guests, at least the younger generation, started asking the same kinds of questions Pete had asked. They were good at getting information. They were subtle. They were sneaky. They teased. But they didn't learn anything.

Eventually we all got past the craziness. Family and friends ended up laughing about my co-workers. They called them 'ghost' people and no members of the project argued. In fact, Mazie told them dead-pan that the word was as good a description as any and later, privately, laughed loud and long at just how accurate the description was.

"Too bad they can never know the truth because we can never tell." Followed by more laughter.

The wedding ended and everyone went back to wherever they'd come from. Family and friends went home. Atlas Project people went back to the facility. And Jack and I went on our honeymoon.

Actually, we weren't sure if it could legitimately be considered a honeymoon or was simply another patrol disguised as a major life event because Thom wanted information on Earth's nearest galactic neighbor.

He decided where we'd go with much gusto and flamboyant gestures with a spoon as he splattered soup all over the kitchen at the facility. Our first patrol as a married couple, he said. Our honeymoon, we told ourselves though he determined the parameters of the trip. What to do. What to look for. What we were supposed to find out while we were there.

We honeymooned on the moon.

Literally.

With Callie, of course, because she'd feel left out if she wasn't along.

And a saucer that saw and heard absolutely

everything though it was nice to know we could call for help in English if something went wrong.

When we landed and had time to ourselves after getting Thom's information, we didn't venture far from the saucer. We could have. The moon doesn't have dust storms. But we didn't.

Just a precaution.

THE END

ABOUT THE AUTHOR

Hi.

I'm Florence Witkop and I love stories.

I love listening to stories. Watching them on TV, video, or movies. Reading them. And writing them.

So I've been a writer since just about forever.

I've written almost every kind of story there is. Mystery, romance, confession, science fiction, fantasy, paranormal, horror, and every other kind I can think of and garnered a few prizes and 'best-selling author' designations along the way.

I've written short stories, novellas, and novels.

In the process I've learned that my favorite stories are action-adventure, science fiction, and paranormal. Preferably the three combined.

My stories are always clean, they are always either contemporary or futuristic, they always have at least a slight romantic element, and they always end happily. Always. Guaranteed. And they all can be read as stand-alone stories even if they are part of a series.

If you want to check out more of my books, click on the link to my website: http://www.FlorenceWitkop.com and read the brief descriptions to see what they are like or click on the link for a more detailed explanation.

My next story is STAR PORTAL in which a young woman goes to a remote area of Wyoming to check out the ranch she and her family inherited. She meets the man from the next ranch over and together they discover a portal to other worlds. As they explore the worlds on the other side of the portal, they realize the possibilities are beyond amazing. But unless they can decipher the strange markings on the portal itself, the return trip isn't guaranteed, and they might be stranded in another universe forever.
STAR PORTAL is a Contemporary Action-Adventure Romance with a generous helping of sci/fi and the paranormal:

STAR PORTAL

by

Florence Witkop

CHAPTER ONE

I stared at the ranch. It had taken more days than necessary to get there because I wasn't sure what I'd find or if I truly wanted to be there. Which was unlike me. I was the adventurous one. That is, I'd always thought of myself as adventurous but now I wasn't so sure.

If I proceeded, my whole life would be totally different from anything I'd ever known. The ranch was remote. Lonely. Empty. The kind of place where anything could happen. And would.

So the closer I got, the slower I drove. When I finally turned off the freeway onto the dirt roads that were all there was beyond civilization, I was barely crawling. When I reached the end of my trip, along what was closer to a cow path than a road, instead of going immediately to what would be my home for the foreseeable future, I stopped. I was tired and my body was screaming for a rest so I used that as an excuse to pull to the side of the seldom-used rutted road and turn off the engine. And just sit.

I stared at the cabin that would be my home for the foreseeable future and let myself remember how it had happened. How I'd actually ended up in such an unlikely place.

***

"You should go," my mother had said in a voice so sweet I knew she had an ulterior motive as she smoothed butter-cream frosting over a sheet cake and set it aside for whomever was going to pick it up for whatever special occasion they were about to celebrate with the help of our family bakery.

"You're the oldest and done with school," she'd said. "You're intelligent and educated. You shouldn't stay with us forever. We can manage without you. You should move out. You should go somewhere and the ranch is as good a place as any to start your adult life. You can spend the whole summer there if you choose. Or forever if you find it's right for you, never to return."

I'd stuck a finger in the left-over frosting and licked it as I listed my many reasons for not going. I shouldn't leave my parents short of help during the busy season. "It's almost summer. Tourists by the dozen. Birthdays, the Fourth of July, and so on. I'm the only one of us kids with no scheduled summer activities and you can't afford to pay someone. So, you need me."

I swiped another finger through the frosting and ignored my mother's frown as I continued. "The younger kids are already scheduled for the entire summer what with baseball, swimming, art and so forth because you believe in a well-rounded education, and I've already done those things but my younger siblings haven't. You can't ask them to give up their summer so I can check out our late uncle's ranch."

I watched to see how she'd react because that reaction could very well decide what I'd be doing that summer. Her expression said my concerns had already been discussed and dealt with. "We'll manage and someone should go, and it must be now because the roads out there are dangerous in the winter and mostly impassible."

I sighed. "Who'd have thought we'd inherit a ranch in Wyoming? It's the end of the world."

My mother sighed along with me. "Inherited with conditions. Like we can't sell it for fifteen years and we suspect your uncle had you in mind when he included that stipulation. There might not have been much visiting between your dad and his brother, but Cantrell was totally interested in his nieces and nephews and always wanted to know what was going on with you kids. So, he knew you're the nature lover. The one who would go bananas over a wild and lonely lifestyle."

"No cell service and no phone."

"So?"

"We'll be unable to communicate. What if something goes wrong?"

"You have gobs of common sense."

"No electricity except for a generator."

"Which you know how to operate."

"Wyoming is far from Illinois and the ranch is isolated." I should stay in Illinois and help with the bakery. But the west was – the west.

The gleam in my mother's eyes said she knew exactly how conflicted I was and that she'd beat down any objections I might have because she and my dad believed in grabbing the brass ring and the ranch in Wyoming was shining brightly with my name writ in large letters. "There's a neighbor. Bridger is the last name, I believe. He's caring for Cantrell's dog."

"Which I'll have to pick up so I'll have to meet him and you're suggesting I casually mention in passing that of course we'll depend on one another. Neighbors and all. With him being the one to provide help and me being the one to need it." I knew my mother and her scheming ways.

She grinned agreement. "Something like that." With which she stuck the frosting bowl in the dishwasher, threw the towels in the laundry and switched off the lights with a finality that meant I was going to Wyoming.

Not too many days later I pulled out of our driveway in the tiny car that had served me well in Illinois and would probably have a panic attack the moment I reached the mountains of Wyoming. It was loaded to the roof with just about everything I owned because none of us had any idea what I'd find when I reached Uncle Cantrell's ranch.

I took a deep breath as I pulled onto the freeway and tried to prepare myself for whatever the summer would bring. I drove carefully, almost sedately, and told myself I was doing so because I was being responsible instead of because my eagerness was mixed with fear of the coming summer alone in a remote area. I didn't know which was stronger. Fear or excitement.

I called home at the last tiny town before reaching the ranch to let everyone know I'd talked with Uncle Cantrell's lawyer and gotten the keys to the cabin. Not that I needed them, he'd said. No one locked their doors. Probably wouldn't even work.

It was my last call before losing cell service so my dad ran me through how to operate the generator that would provide minimal electricity. For the hundredth time. Until he was sure I knew what to do. How to have power. I told him the lawyer said there was plenty of fuel so I didn't need to get any in town. Just groceries.

Then we hung up and I shoved my cell phone in my suitcase, checked the hand-drawn map the lawyer had given me and headed into a region of forested mountains interspersed with open spaces where the wind swept hard and dry across miles of brown terrain.

It didn't feel as though I was climbing but my poor car protested enough that I knew I must be. I slowed down to give the overworked thing a break and to enjoy the scenery with an unexpected feeling of both wonder and freedom that started somewhere in my middle and grew with each curve in the road that opened onto a broad vista of the west.

This wide-open country could be what I'd always wanted. What the entire family knew I wanted even though I'd never said a word. It could be an adventure. That thought competed with an unfamiliar feeling of homesickness that was mixed with a slight touch of fear I'd never expected but couldn't ignore.

I found the ranch easily enough and that was when I stopped far enough away to take a deep breath, reorient myself, and get a good look at the place where I'd be living. It consisted of a small cabin tucked against a hill with a tiny stream crossing what would have been a yard if there'd been anything resembling grass or flowers or any other thing that spoke of civilization. Instead, there was just wilderness and cabin juxtaposed together in perfect harmony with a slightly larger building to one side of the cabin that could have been a barn or tool shed or something else entirely.

Everything appeared neat and well cared for but it was growing late and I had a lot of stuff to lug into the cabin so I started the car once more and decided to check the outbuilding in the morning because now I was hungry and needed to figure out how to make a meal. What kind of stove Uncle Cantrell had used and whether I'd know how to work it. I'd brought lots of sandwich stuff and expected maybe that's what I'd have for dinner.

I parked close to the cabin porch to make unloading easier. Inside I discovered the stove burned wood. I knew how to make a fire because back home we used our fireplace often and roasted marshmallows in the backyard fire pit.

Uncle Cantrell had left the necessary things to get a fire going piled neatly near the stove but far enough away not to be dangerous. Soon I had a fire going that was hot enough for cooking. The heat was welcome because, though it was warm outside, the inside of the cabin was cool enough to make me think the nights might be cold. Summer might come late in the mountains. I didn't know enough about Wyoming to know one way or the other.

I had hot soup for dinner and found the single bedroom clean and comfortable with an assortment of truly warm comforters to choose from that made me wonder just how cold it got in the winter. And maybe all year around. Seeing the blankets, I hesitated before finally deciding to let the fire go out. Surely the comforters would keep me warm.

Still, in an abundance of caution, I piled extra comforters next to the bed to grab if I became chilled during the night. I also put my next day's clothes close enough to grab them and dress beneath the covers if it was really cold. Heavy jeans, boots, a long-sleeved shirt, and a cowboy hat I'd bought in the last town because everyone seemed to be wearing one. Almost as an afterthought, I added a sheepskin vest to the pile. Just in case.

It turned out that the cabin held heat well. Though it was cold outside the next morning, it was warm enough in the cabin that I didn't need the extra comforters or the sheepskin vest. Another fire in the stove to prepare breakfast warmed the entire building enough that I judged it would remain comfortable all day.

The day's outfit had been chosen for whatever I was likely to find in the Wyoming back country. Snakes. Thorny bushes. Sun that felt warm and nice and would burn me to a crisp without sunblock. I'd read about Wyoming.

The cowboy hat had been a good addition to my wardrobe. In short, I was prepared and that made me feel better about the whole thing and suddenly, as I looked through the window to the bright day beyond, in a complete about face from how I'd felt during the trip I felt both competent and adventurous. My parents had been right to push me out of the nest.

The building behind the cabin turned out to be for everything except living. Storage. As a repair shop. It held two large freezers powered by the huge generator I knew how to use thanks to those mini classes from my dad. Diesel fuel was in drums a safe space away from both buildings. No chance of starting either place on fire. My respect for my deceased uncle increased with every new thing I found.

With the place figured out, I turned back to the hand-drawn map with directions to the neighbor's place to pick up Uncle Cantrell's dog. Another place without a phone, most likely, so I couldn't tell him in advance that I was coming. I'd have to just show up and hope he was home.

CHAPTER TWO

I climbed into my tiny car and headed over a low ridge followed by two hills covered with scrubby brush and then still more hills and more brush to my next-door neighbor's place. A lot of miles, I decided, and wondered if long distances were common between ranches in this remote part of Wyoming. But the scenery was lovely, wild and stark, and I drove slowly enough to take it all in.

I'd been there less than a full day and had already decided I wanted Wyoming to become a part of me. To sink into my soul. I was an introvert, and this place was made for solitude. Hermits welcome, adventure would be an added perk that seemed to be waiting around every curve in the road.

The ranch where I was to pick up Uncle Cantrell's dog was almost a duplicate of the ranch I'd just left, only slightly larger. A cabin with one outbuilding but this outbuilding was considerably larger than my uncle's. Maybe large enough to be a barn and there was a lean-to on the back of it that was as large as my uncle's entire second building that could serve the same function as that entire second building on Uncle Cantrell's ranch. Or more. But the cabin itself was about the same size.

I drove close to the cabin and parked in what I hoped was an acceptable spot but I couldn't know because, like at Uncle Cantrell's ranch, there was no defined yard and no discernable parking area. Just bare ground with wild grasses that were green and yellow and brown with rocks strewn about here and there. The result was lovely in a way I'd not thought could possibly be lovely. But it was.

I got out and wondered where to start looking for the owner. I needn't have bothered because my car engine had hardly died when a man stepped out of the cabin. Tallish, muscular from outdoor living with brown hair that needed a haircut and a totally male no-nonsense, put-together way about him. He was wearing clothes that were a duplicate of what I wore. Jeans, boots, and a long-sleeved shirt. I was sure there was a cowboy hat somewhere in the cabin that he'd grab before he went anywhere.

"Hi," he said in a pleasant baritone. No hint of an accent so no way to know where he was from. "You here for the dog?"

"How'd you know?"

"Easy enough." He laughed, a comfortable sound in the crystal air that invited me to relax. How'd he see that I was nervous? And why was I? There was no reason for it. I was a normal person on a normal errand. But I felt somehow weird in the wide-open land and now I knew my nerves were obvious to anyone who looked. Unless his acuity was a Wyoming thing. Perhaps the solitude made inhabitants better able to read their occasional guests.

My face flushed as I realized he was standing there reading me like a book, emotions and all. Then he explained how he knew who I was. "You're driving a tiny car that can only be from a city and the family that inherited Cantrell's ranch is from a city. Somewhere in Illinois, I believe. So it wasn't hard to figure out who you are. Besides, I don't get a lot of company. No one does out here."

His head tilted a bit as he added, "This country doesn't lend itself to people wandering all over the place. But I knew someone would come eventually to get Midnight."

"Midnight? Is that the dog's name?" I considered his expression from when he first saw me. My new neighbor might be a nice man. A decent person. Then I felt stupid because of course he was a decent person. He was caring for my uncle's dog, and he didn't have to do that. "You're right. I'm here for Uncle Cantrell's dog."

"Midnight is around someplace. He likes to go exploring. He might have gone somewhere. He could be gone a while."

"I can come back later."

"No need. If I'd known you were coming to get him today, I'd have kept him in the barn but, unfortunately, without a phone there was no way to know when it would happen." A smile flashed across his face. White teeth gleamed briefly. "Come on in. I can make a pot of coffee if you drink coffee and I think I have some cookies if they haven't gone stale."

"I love coffee." I didn't care if the cookies were stale. I was in Wyoming. I'd made it here and I was talking with a real, live cowboy and could spend the whole summer here if I chose. Or forever. As I followed him into the cabin, I found myself thinking I just might do that. In fact, I might do more. I might become a cowgirl myself if such was possible.

"I'm Noah," he said over strong, hot, black coffee and cookies that were sort of edible.

"Emma."

We studied each other. Now that we were out of the bright sun and close enough to see details I saw sun-browned skin and hands rough from physical work but the thing I noticed most was an alertness, as if he saw everything about his surroundings in an instant and tucked that information away somewhere to be pulled out as needed.

There was nothing special about me for him to see. Longish brown hair and everything else as medium as possible. I was the epitome of normal and fidgeted under his inspection. He, on the other hand, improved with each new thing I noticed. His height, the way his head tilted, and his eyes sparked with intelligence and the fact that he didn't gesture much when he spoke. But though he seemed totally relaxed, it was the stillness of a coiled spring.

My mother had been right. This man could be a handy person to know. He definitely gave out competent vibes and I was glad he'd be nearby if serious problems arose though I'd never ask for help for anything less than an actual catastrophe. Not my style. I'm determinedly self-sufficient.

But it was hard to pull my eyes away until I realized I was staring way longer than was polite. Then I flushed and forced myself to look over the inside of the cabin. As neat as Uncle Cantrell's place, with what must be a bedroom as the only other room and open shelves everywhere filled with the necessities of life in the country.

The whole time I checked him over and after I'd looked away, his eyes examined me. I could feel them on me and decided to take the focus off me by putting it on him. "What do you do so far from everywhere? Do you own cattle?" A normal assumption in the rural west.

He didn't act like I was being nosy, merely shook his head. "Not cattle. Horses. I'm okay with horses and a fair rider so I train horses and teach riders how to ride better."

"Like a rodeo person?"

"Just normal riding. For cattle roundups and

pleasure." His eyes sparked. "I like horses and I like people as long as there aren't too many of them at any one time."

A good person to know indeed. If my brand-new goal of becoming a cowgirl was to be filled, he was the place to start.

I lapsed into silence but he continued to look at me. He had something on his mind and it wasn't horses. I learned what it was when he said, "It's none of my business but I have a question if you don't mind."

"What do you want to know?"

"Your uncle was a nice guy. A good neighbor. I liked him a lot. But he seemed to have a secret."

"Uncle Cantrell? A secret?" I turned over what I knew about the uncle I'd only seen a few times during my life. "I don't know what it could have been. He wasn't a felon. Or hiding from anyone."

He got up and moved about the single room, pouring himself another cup of coffee before sitting down once more and replacing his feet on a chair in an impression of ease that wouldn't fool anyone. "It's probably nothing. It's just an impression I got that there was more to him than what could be seen. I was wondering if you know what it was." It was clear he truly believed my late uncle had been hiding something.

"Sorry but I know nothing about any secret and I'm sure no one in our family knows anything either." By then I was curious. "Did he give any indication what kind of secret it was?"

He shook his head. "Nope. Nothing. And maybe I was just imagining it. Maybe it was just his personality and there was no secret." But his expression said Uncle Cantrell had been hiding something.

A sound interrupted us. A scratching at the door. "Here's Midnight." He opened the door and in walked the largest black Labrador retriever I'd ever seen in my life who looked me over and started towards me but stopped a few feet away. "Here," Noah said, tossing me a broken piece of cookie. "Give it to him. He's a foodie and he'll love you forever."

Soon Midnight and I were friends. "Thanks,"

"No thanks needed. Midnight is a good doggie. And a sweetheart."

"He's huge."

"The biggest Lab I've ever seen."

"Everything out here seems to be big."

That smile again and a chuckle. "I guess Wyoming is different than where you're from."

"Totally."

He studied me some more only this time the look was completely friendly. The initial inspection was done. I hoped we were friends. A friend would be nice, possibly essential. "Do you ride?"

"Huh?"

"Horses? Do you ride horses?"

"Yes, but I doubt my skill level would be considered acceptable around here." Our neighbors had horses and loved kids so all the kids in the neighborhood learned the fundamentals. But I'd never gotten further than that. I wasn't a cowgirl. Yet.

"It's early. Lots of daytime left. We can go for a ride if you like. You can get to know the countryside. I can show you around your property." He stopped, then continued, "If you want. If you have the time."

"I'd like that." And of course, I had time. Time stretched open and inviting in this land that felt disconnected from the rest of the world. Midnight begged for another cookie, and I gave him a second piece. "But what about Midnight?"

"He can come too. He'll love it." He examined the huge Lab so big he could have been part horse. "He'll be good to have along. Large, competent, and protective of his people." He looked at me over his coffee. "Which will be you once he gets to know you better. A ride will be a good time for the two of you to start the process." With which he grabbed the wide-brimmed cowboy hat I knew had to be somewhere in the cabin, plopped it on his head, strapped a pistol around his waist, and led the way outside.

Turned out the second building was a barn, as I'd thought. Several empty stalls because the horses were outside, several western saddles and a lot of tack along one side. A couple of cats watched from the loft. "I'll get the horses."

"Are they far away?"

"In the corral." I flushed. I'd not noticed the wire fence behind the barn and the horses were in a thicket of evergreen trees so I'd not seen them either. "They like the shade." He opened the corral gate and walked through. I followed. "You can wait here if you want."

"I'd like to go with you." The cowgirl thing. If I was to learn how to do cowgirl things this was a good time to start my education as well as a good time to get close to Midnight. "Get to know the horse I'll be riding," I added, as if an explanation was needed, but it was the truth.

I wasn't a good enough rider to climb on board just any horse and have it go where it was told. I was glad Noah would be around if it decided to go somewhere else. Mostly I hoped his look of competency wasn't an act and that his horses were well trained.

They were. I suspected he picked the most laid-back one for me, a pinto named Cutie Pie with a straight back and a rocking gate that put me at ease. As we headed into the scrub brush that seemed to be the entirety of the nearby landscape, I patted her neck. She replied with a comfortable grunt and didn't speed up even a little bit which was fine with me.

The day was warm, the sun bright, the breeze perfect and I enjoyed every moment of the trip. We rode the boundary of my new property. Then we rode the boundary of Noah's ranch. "Is it all scrub brush?"

"Not all. There are some interesting rock formations not far from here. They are mostly on your property though some are on mine. Your uncle said the area reminded him of days gone by. Before the area was settled." He turned his horse towards a formation a short ride away.

Cutie Pie followed without me having to do anything. She was a nice, sweet horse. A docile follower. Thankfully. "It'll be level ground one minute and rocks thirty feet high the next and they'll look like they are stuck one on top of another. As if they were dropped from the sky and that was how they landed."

We reached the rocks, and they did, indeed, stand out in stark contrast to the surrounding area. The horses stopped as if they made this trip often and knew when we'd arrived. They started grazing on the sparse grass. I started to dismount but Noah put out a hand, reaching across the space between us, and stopped me. "Let me make sure it's safe."

I looked around. "Safe from what?"

"Whatever. Cougars, possibly. More likely rattlesnakes." He rode next to a boulder taller than his horse and scooped up a handful of small rocks that he threw around. "Chasing away any snakes." I was glad he was there and finally realized why he had a pistol strapped to his waist. For whatever happened to be around. I had a lot to learn about life out west.

I didn't dismount until after Noah was off his horse and had walked around a bit. Then I climbed down gingerly and looked around and only moved away from trusty Cutie Pie after I'd thoroughly inspected the nearby ground. It seemed okay and the fact that Midnight was nosing around all over the place gave me confidence that there were no nasty surprises ready to jump out at me.

I joined Noah and ignored his almost-smile at my tenderfoot ways. "You were right. The rocks are interesting." I went up to the closest one. Scrub brush covered most of it and prevented me from getting right next to it. But I could look.

I pointed. "That formation in the rock. It's shaped like a door."

*So now you know how **Star Portal** begins. If you want to find out what happens next and how it ends, click on the link to my website http://www.FlorenceWitkop.com where you will find a link to it on Amazon.*